I0735887

CONSUMMATION

Stories

Blake Edward Hamilton

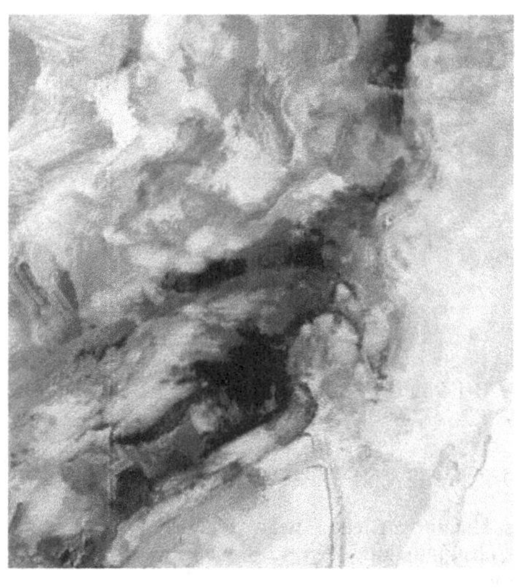

SPUYTEN DUYVIL

NEW YORK CITY

The Exchange was originally published on National Public Radio.

© 2023 Blake Edward Hamilton
ISBN 978-1-959556-33-6

Library of Congress Cataloging-in-Publication Data

Names: Hamilton, Blake Edward, author.
Title: Consummation : stories / Blake Edward Hamilton.
Description: New York City : Spuyten Duyvil, 2023.
Identifiers: LCCN 2023012932 | ISBN 9781959556336 (paperback)
Subjects: LCGFT: Short stories.
Classification: LCC PS3608.A666 C66 2023 | DDC 813/.6--dc23/
eng/20230515
LC record available at https://lccn.loc.gov/2023012932

For
My teachers
For
My Mom

CONTENTS

Consummation

THE DELIVERY

There are roads heading into vast nowheres all over this place, but you can still see the red, like blood filling up a glass of water, right at the lines of things when the sun goes down. My trip from Barstow to Las Cruces, New Mexico is cut short at around 4:00 AM. Driving from the West, it's as far as I get, which is why I'm at this hulking 12 pump monster for truckers in the desert surrounded by black night on all sides. I got the brown Buick my brother gave me parked at the back end of the parking lot, which stretches so far that it's good enough for an airplane, but back here are just the truckers stationed overnight, sleeping in their cabins or jacking off to porn; and I sometimes see legs sliding out of cabin doors, dangling, then dropping down, followed by the click-clack of heels echoing down the tiny alleys created by long trailers hauling deliveries. A lot of meat trucks, maybe. I have a delivery, too, except mine can't be seen or talked about. It's what I promised. 75,000 in cash to deliver a box. No idea what's in the box, but it's enough to carry with one arm, and it's in the trunk under a bunch of blankets. I didn't ask, but I made a promise, and if I can get it to Las Cruces by 8:00 PM this coming day, I'll be doing my brother a favor; he doesn't tell me what kind of business it is, or how he got into it, or what it means if this box never makes it, but he is clear that he doesn't have anyone else, and that if it doesn't happen, well, then that is it, and I'm not going to let my brother go in some awful way, not when I can help it, and it's just a drive, a simple desert drive with no one around, and just the stars out. I can smoke with the window down, he says, so that's what I do. Once I hit Barstow from Vegas, however, two tires go out, and it's the back right and the front left.

The truckers are sleeping and no one inside can help me. I'm leaning against this fucking Buick, smoking, and I don't know what to do until I see a woman in her thirties, maybe forties, I can't tell, but her hair is a pile of blond curls, and she's got a fringe jean jacket on, red pumps, red mouth. She gets out of her dark blue Ford sedan to go inside, and she leaves the window down and the car running. Jesus, lady, I'm thinking, I'm your worst enemy, and I'm right here. So I get the box out of the trunk, hold it carefully in my right arm, some blankets folded on top, and I grab some small stuff from the Buick. I start walking fast to the girl's sedan. It's only a few steps away, really. I come out of the dark part of the lot and into the bright lights overhead. I pull the latch and slide right into the driver's seat, the car purring. I put the box and blankets on the passenger side and scoot the seat forward, gripping the wheel. I look over the blue dashboard to search for the woman inside. I can see the top of her blond head moving down the aisles, her back to the windows. She probably thinks she'll just run in, be real quick, and look what happens.

I put the car in reverse, back out, then speed off to the highway. I only get a few hundred miles before the engine stalls, and I have to ditch the car on the shoulder. I wait for a while until a guy in overalls with no shirt underneath picks me up in a beater; this truck is slashes of faded red on top of faded gray, and the inside is covered in deep brown everywhere, and it smells like cheap cherry-flavored cigarillos. Man, he talks a lot about nothing, just blabs about shit, like how to deep fry a steak or where he went in the war, and how, thank

God, we live here in America because here we're safe from things like cult extremists and illness, or even dictators. He asks me if I've seen *The Conversation*, a Coppola movie. It's 1977, so the movie's already a bit old. He's not very consistent and drops threads of talk before moving on to other stories. I pretend to listen as he blabs because it's the least I can do since he's giving me a ride, and I plan to steal his truck, like I stole the woman's sedan earlier. He pulls off the highway 'to piss,' he says, and he finds a back road and a turn off to a darker area. He gets out, waddles down to a small ditch, and disappears somewhere in the dark, and I can't see him. I wait a minute, the truck thrumming, and then I slide over to take the wheel. I put the truck into reverse, back out, and then head to the highway. I check the rearview to see if the guy will come running after me, but only dirt and gravel lit red by the rear of the truck cloud up behind me as I drive. The guy is nowhere.

Back on the highway, I only stop once for gas, and keep the box on the floorboard of the passenger seat. Glancing down at it a few times in the orange glow of the radio, I can only make out one edge. I want to open it, just a quick peek. Why's this thing so important? I want to ask my brother, should have asked, but I know better. It's easier to pretend the thing's not there; that I'm just driving, just taking a trip, which I am, and the rest of the desert spreads out around me. I'm driving for hours when I cross the Arizona border. The sun's coming up, red and yellow at the same time, and all around me is orange. The wide expanse of bluffs come toward the truck as I speed further on. The highway asphalt snakes away into orange dirt, a black tail, and cactuses stand bent under a blue sky filling with giant clouds. Cotton-white and full, they look like a bunch of rags covering something up.

•

The sky takes on a purple color later in the day and seems to soak up some of the orange in the dirt and the strange green of the cactuses everywhere. It's a shade of green the way a stone would be green. Some even look blue the farther away they are. Sometimes I think I see figures moving around out there, walking across the orange dirt, but it's just tall cactus bodies. The road moves through this terrain for a while when I start to get hungry and realize I don't have anything, not even a bag of chips, just my brother's damn box and a pile of useless blankets.

A town has to pop up soon somewhere, I tell myself, a little town out here; I imagine a few of them will appear on this damn highway. Even a Ma and Pa shop will do. It's another hour of driving and feeling like my stomach is caving in that I finally see one of these places, a combo Ma and Pa place with a Texaco. There's an old time, glass bottle Coke machine next to a white bench out front. I smell smoke in the air, like wood chips burning in a grill. I pull up to one of the pumps, put the car into park and turn off the engine. The place is moderately populated. Looks like a few ranch hands in plaid shirts and dusty hats, a couple of kids with a woman in a pink shirt covering large, swinging breasts, and a brown stack of coiffed hair on her head. I grab a sandwich from one of the coolers, a bag of chips, and a six pack of Coors. Back in the truck I wolf it all down and chug two Coors, and belch so loud with the window down that the woman with kids shoots me a look of disgust as she exits the store, heading around the corner to a junker with stuffed animals in the back window. *Bitch*, I think, and want to say, but don't, trying to avoid as much trouble as possible. When I turn on the engine and sit back into the seat, I realize how tired I am, suddenly. My back feels numb in places, and I need a real bed. Glancing at the box on the floorboard, I put the truck into drive and pull back onto the highway, the sun burning right through the streaked windshield, baking the plastic dashboard into a fine chemical smell all through everything. I can smell a mix of old bodies, a faint whiff of sour perfume, old air fresheners. The memory of this car is something I've stolen as well. When you steal something, you never just take the thing; you take its entire life, every history that came with it. In fact, you don't really steal anything but what a thing was, not what it's becoming, and not what it might be. What history have I stolen now, I wonder?

The radio in the truck picks up an old jazz station and a bleak trumpet pours out across the desert in front of me, hotter now with the sun getting stronger. The truck's engine growls up the road as the land shifts, changing shape every which way. The trumpet is a lonely whisper, and the road has no cars. Nothing passes me for hours. It's around 9:30 AM that I see him, the walker on the side of the road. He's in white pants rolled up to the calves and wears a white shirt, loose on his body, like a curtain against a wall, and he's got a blue and green striped pack slung over his shoulder; his left arm is out with his hand up, his hitcher thumb pointing straight toward the clouds. His back is to me, and he has a lot of dark hair close to his shoulders. When I get closer I notice he's barefoot. I'm stunned for a moment, looking right at his bare, white feet against the hot asphalt, the rocks and gravel there, and maybe even old needles blown in from cactuses. What is this man doing out here hitching barefoot and walking like he's on something soft?

Picking up a hitcher in my circumstances is not the best plan in the world, but I sympathize with the man, oddly, and what's a quick ride gonna do? I need the company anyway, and it could help me sleep a bit; the guy looks gentle, like he might get torn apart by a mountain lion if he stays out here. I decide I'm doing him and me a favor by picking him up. I turn off the radio, wave through the window, and pull to the side of the road a ways ahead, and for a minute I can't see the guy anymore. I look in the rearview, and he should be walking up, but when I turn to the passenger side window, he's already at the truck, smiling at me through the dirt-streaked glass. The window's partly rolled down, so I can hear him.

"You going east?" he asks me, adjusting the pack on his shoulder.

"I am, hop in."

He mutters thanks, and opens the door, then slides

onto the seat, his feet on either side of the box on the floor. I tell him he can put his feet on the blankets on top of the box, which he does, and I speed back onto the highways. For a minute he's quiet, just looking through the windshield at the passing desert. I can't help looking at this feet again. They're milk-white and speckled in dried mud that somehow makes them whiter. The Achilles tendon of his left foot has a large circular scab as if someone put a long nail through it. Little lines of dried blood trickle down from the wound, coating the edge of his foot as if he stepped into brown ink. I ask him what happened to his foot. He looks at me but doesn't say anything. I tell him he's welcome to a beer. I pull one off for myself and drink it down pretty quick, hoping this drive won't become awkward, now.

"How long have you been out there?" I gesture to the scenery.

He shrugs. "I don't know. I've only known this road. A while, I guess."

"You mean you've only been hitching here? Nowhere else?"

"No, I've been all over, just can't remember where."

"Are you from Arizona?"

"Yeah, a town."

"What brings you out here? If I can ask. Where you going?"

"I used to know. I"m just hitching."

"No trajectory, huh?"

"I'm just on this road."

"I hear ya, man."

"What about you? Why are you on this road?" he asks.

"I've got a delivery to make. Gotta be there pretty soon."

"Must be important."

"You might say that."

"Is it this package here?" he asks, and taps the box with his white left toe.

I nod, and try to change the subject.

"Had any luck out here?"

"There was one guy, but I only got so far."

"You're my first hitcher."

"How's that working out for you?"

"So far, so good. I just don't know how you're making it on bare feet. Where'd your shoes go?"

"They're just my feet."

"Someone take them from you?"

"They're gone."

"Well, I can see that."

"Gotta name?"

"Lukas."

I introduce myself, tell him it's nice to meet him, and that he's welcome to tag along as far as he wants to go, even if it's across the state line. I mention how I'd be grateful if he'd like to drive for a bit, but when I look over, he's asleep against the door, curled up almost, the soles of his feet exposed to me, and the left one is completely black as if painted with tar.

When he wakes up, he adjusts himself in the seat, then kicks the box accidentally, and I look to make sure it's all right. Then I notice the guy is sporting a huge, hard dick in his pants, poking right up under the pant seam. He seems almost unaware of it, but it's difficult not to notice. I clear my throat and try to focus on the road. I look back at him and it's still there, pushing toward his stomach. Then I catch him looking right at me, a subtle smile on his face, the face of a twenty-something. My gut tells me to apologize, but I don't say anything. I just stare ahead at the road, and hope he'll do something about it.

"I'm sorry," he says. "Sometimes happens."

"S'alright. I get it, man."

"Were you looking? I saw you looking. Were you curious?"

"No, I'm—I'm just driving."

"I don't blame you if you are. Here, see? It is oddly bigger than normal."

The guy, Lukas, pulls down the flap of his white pants and flops out his cock, all full-up hard, and it just tilts to the side in the bright light of the day. My throat goes all tight and dry, and I turn my attention back to the road again. But he keeps talking with his dick out.

"Big, I know. I sometimes don't even feel like its mine. Just this big ol' dick."

I don't respond, but clear my throat again. I scratch my arm, wishing I had some cigarettes, and think of my dad, our ugly front yard with dry, dead grass in our vacant neighborhood full of empty, unsold houses. *You ever get an urge, son, you take one of these, see, smoke it till the coal's real hot, and you give yourself a crater, right there in the arm, just roll up yer sleeve, and push the coal in. It'll hurt like a motherfucker, but it'll stop you from wantin'. See, look at my arm. It's like the moon.*

I've got two craters in my arm. One from high school years, and one much later, but I run my fingers over the toughened skin there. *And you're gonna need to fight, son. I'm tellin' you what no one told me. At first you gotta force yourself. You aren't gonna like it, but you gotta; that's how I have you. I forced it. Force yourself until you do like it. And if your eyes wander, you know what to do. I'm tell-*

ing you this cause I see myself in you. Remember, like the moon. Just do what I tell you.

When I look back at Lukas, he's asleep again. I turn the radio back on, and the trumpet has been replaced by another slow tune, someone strumming bass, a piano behind it. I roll down the window and the desert air hits my face, and I'm drinking it in like it's water. My nervous system feels like its hit with something electric, and my shoulders drop, my neck lets loose. I have two beers left, and I gulp both down pretty quickly, and feel a little like I'm too light afterwards. The steering wheel feels like paper in my fingers, and my gums are swollen against my molars. My spine aches for a mattress. When Lukas wakes up a second time, he smiles at me from the corner of the door, his head against the window.

"Want to make some money?" he asks. I look at him, not saying anything, but hoping he'll elaborate.

He sits up, points over the dashboard. "Just over there a few miles off a backroad called Townsend is an old house. It's been left. No one's there, obviously, but there's money buried out there. A whole case of it. I know because it's my family's, and they left it."

"Don't you want it?" I ask him. "Seems to me you could use it."

"No, I don't want it. I have no need for it."

"Just a man of the road, huh?"

"I am here."

"So why tell me about this money, then? Why me?"

"Why anyone? If you don't want it, that's fine. Someone will find it."

"How much are we talking?"

"A quarter of a million, maybe. Perhaps more."

"Quarter of a million dollars in an abandoned house a few miles that way. You gotta be kidding."

"Just right over there."

I wait a moment, gauging his sincerity. And then I understand, he's serious. And maybe he's being honest, but I'm not sold enough, yet.

"We're about to pass it. If you're gonna do it, do it now."

"Where? Where is it?" I ask him. And then there's a small road, a tiny slit to the left, the road sign leaning like the cactuses. He points again, arm almost in my face, and I'm turning left, straight down the dirt road alongside a barbed wire fence. The truck bucks over potholes in the road, and the axle whines underneath. I bounce in my seat as the wheels cut across the ground, swooping over empty nothing everywhere.

"You better not be lying. And this better not be an

ambush. I've got some place to be, and I've gotta haul ass to get there."

"I think you'll enjoy this," is all he says, his eyes oddly flat and unreflective in the sunlight.

"It's just up here," he says, and points again, and I see it, a tiny, collapsing farm house. One of those many shattered, leaning devastations left to the elements. A place someone lived in once, but now it's just limp boards, windows without glass, open to derelict rooms. All around it the earth is pounded flat and an old drive is visible where I pull in and park at a diagonal from what used to be a porch that has crumbled into the dirt. Rotting boards fan outward. I stay in the truck for a minute, staring at it, looking for movement of any kind, and there's nothing. Just this empty place looking cold under the sun, like it's trying to remember what it is.

"Okay. Okay, let's do this. Let's make it quick. Where's this money?" I ask him. I turn off the car, then start to open the door and step into the dirt.

"I'll show you. It's a great day for this."

"It's something."

"Follow me."

I hear him get out of the car, and I listen to his feet in the dirt for a minute, and then I catch what I think is his shadow, or the shape of him moving up along the side of the house really quick. I hurry over and try to follow, running along the right, then around toward the back, and he's not there. I call out his name, and the wind answers, a hard, cold shove from across the desert behind us. I call his name again and the house creaks in response, a low clacking sound, something like a glass bottle rolling around inside there somewhere. I step closer to it, and there's a missing back door, just an opening right inside, and when I look, it's only empty rooms. I don't see Lukas.

Maybe the money is off the property somewhere, or buried a few miles out. I turn and scan the horizon, the empty rooms of the house to my back. I call for Lukas, but the wind just howls down, and my shirt flutters against my skin, cold and sharp. Nothing is there. I walk around the house a couple of times, and Lukas is nowhere, the crazy bastard. Where the fuck did he go? My lungs feel raw from shouting, from the cold air despite the sun, and I head back to the truck. Lukas isn't there either. I get in and start the engine. The canted face of the old house hangs forward; its weather-beaten facade rattles in the wind. How old can it be? 60? 70 years old? Maybe more. I roll down the window a bit, and search for Lukas through the grimy glass. Then I honk the horn a few times, and still nothing. Dumb son of a bitch. Maybe he went on. Looking down at the floorboard I see the box is still there, but his pack is gone. I back out, slowly, and turn the truck around to go the way we came when I almost run right over him, standing at the side of the road, hand out, hitcher thumb up, and a smile on his face. He has his pack with him. What kind of a joke is this? I pull up and he climbs in, putting his bare feet right on the blankets, like before. He rubs his hands together.

"It's a sudden cold wind outside. Damn this desert. Where are we headed?"

"You're a real prankster. Let me tell you."

"Where are we headed?"

"There was no money out there, was there?"

"Only money I need is right here." He taps his chest, the spot over his heart.

"That's good, Lukas."

When we get back to the main thoroughfare, I hit the gas hard, making up for the time I slaughtered back at that abandoned shack, and hope I can still make it to New Mexico in time. I don't feel too bad about it, but only have periods for smaller stops, now, if that. And Lukas, with his big dick, is asleep against the door again, knees curled up. He seems to not take up space while also taking up space. His skin is the same flat color, and light doesn't appear to mingle with it, like the road got him and made him a part of it, took him into itself. His color is the color of everything scattered along it, as if they absorbed one another.

We drive on, and I don't get the break I hoped for, but Lukas is still company of a kind. I rub the spot on my arm a few times, knowing better, and the tightness in my gut passes. It's been there a while, pulling everything inside me into a knot, my bones, all of it; my body is crushing itself from the inside with this tension. But when it's gone, I can concentrate on the road, the driving, the relief I'll feel when I get this box delivered, and whatever's inside it.

●

When we pass Phoenix and get near Tuscon, Lukas says he has another place he wants to show me.

"I appreciate the sight seeing and all, but I can't really afford the detours right now."

"How much time do you need?"

"At the moment, at this rate, I should be there with a few hours to kill."

"Then you've got time for this."

"Another abandoned house?"

"Not at all."

"What, then?"

"You'll just have to trust me."

"I suppose that's possible. But let me think on it."

"Where did you go back there?"

"I don't understand."

"The house. Or whatever it was. You just kind of went away."

"I know no houses," he says this, and seems weighed suddenly, like he's been walloped with a strange sadness.

"Well, I called out to you."

He doesn't say anything, just stares at the passing cactuses.

"You didn't hear me?"

A few minutes go by and Lukas seems resigned to saying nothing now. And for about an hour, we ride in silence. Occasionally, the radio breaks it up.

"I think there might be time."

"Time?"

"To stop. What's this place you mentioned?"

"You want to see the place?"

"That's what I'm saying. Let's do it. Show me the place."

Lukas nods as if to signal that I've made the right

decision, although I can't be sure I am making any decisions I'll be able to live with at this stage. I feel bound to this road somehow.

"But you have to tell me something if I agree to this."

"What do you want to know?"

I point at his foot. "What happened there? To your tendon. There's obviously something wrong there. Looks like it needs peroxide and maybe a tetanus shot."

Lukas peers at it, bemused almost, then a bit of confused regret in his features, an expression like the house back there.

"Did someone do that to you? An animal? What punctured your heel?"

"I remember metal," he says. "I remember cold."

Then there is silence again as he looks at it. He runs his index finger around the raw edges of the hole.

"Wherever we stop, I think we should get you something to treat that."

"I remember how it felt. How scared I was cause I knew it was over. There was nothing I could do."

"Are you talking about a person."

"I never saw him. But I knew he was there."

"Knew who was there?"

"It was quick. It was quick."

I tell him I'll take his word for it, and an hour and a

half later he says we're near the place he's mentioned. On either side of the truck is more desert, but there's a small road leading off the highway that takes us to a town called Doumont. Three buildings and a gas station. Some kind of odd professional, single-level office building. And a few miles down, there is a tiny grade school; the playground is empty. Around the corner a few streets over is a small neighborhood. The houses are probably from the late 40s, maybe the late 60s. This place has died out, and there isn't much to recommend it. I struggle to understand why Lukas has brought us here. Behind the neighborhood further on is a cemetery, a library, and a closed hamburger joint with paintings of freckle-faced kids playing jump rope with a dog on the side of the building. A bubble coming out of the boy's mouth says, 'Boy, howdy! Gimme some of those treats!' A bubble out of the girl's mouth reads, simply, 'Golly, gee!' The dog is leaping at nothing, just hovering in the air, mouth open, ready to bite or bark, but there's nothing for him to catch. Just a vacancy in his wide, exaggerated eyes.

An old woman at a house down at the end of the street stands outside, angrily throwing cans of paint against the sides of it, screaming. At the intersection, a small child in a cloth diaper plays in the dirt. Once we leave most of the town behind us, looming ahead is a stretch of road that appears to go further out into the desert, but up ahead I can see something glimmering, something white and tall, like a billboard, but blank. A few minutes later, and we're at an entrance to a closed drive-in movie theater from the 50s. We pull in and see the rows of poles where cars can park, and the giant screen is right in front, bigger than a billboard. Its surface catches the sun and shoots it back to us. I steer the truck over to one of the old slots. Tall, dry weeds stand out of cracks all over the place, some waving in the wind. The snack shack behind us has a white wooden board slanted across the order window. Faded paintings like the hamburger shop flank both sides of it, only these are giant lollipops and popcorn boxes with legs and faces. The sucker has something to say, unlike the dog: 'Open me up, and lick me good! Mmm delicious!' A pickle a few feet over says something similar, while pushing his engorged head through an unzipped bag.

Lukas is held by the screen. He seems to beam at it, his face happier than I've seen it since I picked him up hours ago. A tearful joy shapes his eyes. He grips the edge of the door with his hand, and his knee with the other. He looks like he's going to burst right through the windshield and fly straight to the screen. I can say anything to him now and it won't matter. I don't think he will hear me, or anyone. I could ask him what this place is, but what a ridiculous question. A better question is what is this place to Lukas? Why drive all the way here? What history is still here for him? I start to ask him some version of these questions, but just stare at the blank screen along with him. I roll down my window and listen to the hollow clanking of chains on poles, the brittle rattle of sagebrush in the fields beyond the screen, the top right of which is caved inward, producing a hole that reveals the other side, a slice of blue sky and the start of a rocky bluff.

"I'll be right back," I tell Lukas. "I gotta piss."

I step out of the truck and find a corner over by the giant lollipop and pickle. I unzip and cover the cracked, white paint on the edges of the old snack shop with a heavy stream. Far back in the corner is a couple of trashcans that look like they haven't been moved in twenty years, and some boxes wilted around them. I see movement down below, a jitter of light. A head pokes out. It's a possum, and it darts back into its makeshift cave when it sees me. A baby possum pokes out for a minute, too. I zip up my brown trousers and make my way to the truck. Lukas isn't sitting in it. He's all the way up near the screen.

"Hey, Lukas, we gotta go!"

He either doesn't hear me or doesn't respond, or both, but I honk the horn, and it makes no difference.

"Hey, Lukas!"

There's a tap on the back of the truck. I turn around to see what it is and an old, hunched man is there, looking right at me. His jaw pushes forward, and he squints.

"Who you callin'?" he asks me.

"Sorry, just my friend up there, Lukas."

"There ain't no one there. Just you, making a disturbance."

"I'm sorry. Do you live around here, or something?"

"This my home."

"The theater?"

"This," and he jerks his elbow at the snack shack.

"You been living here? How long?"

"Since I owned it. Since it closed. Now git outta here."

"I will. Once I get my friend."

"I told you, there ain't no one here! Now git."

"I think you're mistaken, sir, my friend—"

And when I look back to the drive-in screen, I see that he is right. There is no one. Lukas isn't anywhere.

"I'm sorry, I'll be right back. My friend tends to wander."

"Listen," he says, and grabs hold of my arm. "You can git, or you can stand around all day and night. It don't make any difference. I'm telling you, there ain't no one."

"What do you mean?"

"My son, he bring 'em all here. At one time or another, he bring 'em."

"What do you mean, *your* son?"

"He comes home every once in a while."

I don't say anything, waiting for him to hurry up.

"They ain't got any other way. They need people, like you, to bring 'em."

"Well, the guy I'm with is a twenty-year-old living in his own world, and I feel kind of responsible for him right now."

"That's what he'd be if he was found. But my son is old. He's old."

I turn away from him and try calling again. "Lukas!"

"He ain't there, mister. I'm tellin' ya. He just ain't there. He's gone."

"I don't know what you mean."

"He been gone. Many years now. They ain't ever find him. But sometimes he come home. Sometimes he come home. Just his way. Understand?"

I felt something cold go over me standing there in

front of this old man with skin that hung on him, white and freckled, his forehead wrinkling. I nodded at him. It was all I could do.

"Go on, now," he says. "You done enough."

•

When I pull into Las Cruces, it's like a ghost town. No one's around, except a few cars, but I don't see any people. Dirt and pebbles smack against the side of the truck in a wind that comes in hard gusts, just like someone pushing against the car from all directions, unseen. Dirt and dead sagebrush blow into the middle of the road. The mountains ahead take on a yellow haze from the sun, rising up like broken teeth jutting forward. I pass a Motel 6, then further on to Downtown, which looks dead. The address on the box is in my brother's handwriting, a mechanical style in black felt-tip. I spot a corner pharmacy. The lights are on inside, so I pull over. Inside is an old man with dark hair and deeply wrinkled skin behind the white counter next to a spin rack of paperbacks. He's quick when I ask him for directions. An impatient woman in a white raincoat with a clear plastic wrap over hair sprayed into a dome, taps her foot behind me. The pharmacist appears to know her; he groans when he leaves me to tend to her. Before I go, I buy a pack of cigarettes, then hurry back to the truck.

I take the roads given to me, and it's a long path all the way through old neighborhoods to the west of the mountains. The pharmacist says the place is about twenty minutes out from Downtown. The streets remain empty, even though I wish I saw someone; my chest begins to clench itself the more I drive, the more the streets show no people. I don't know why, it just does. I light a cigarette, smoke half of it, then drop it from the window.

The location of the address is a small house on a property way back from the road with a gate that says WHEELER RANCH on it. Sagebrush pocks the yard, which is mostly dirt. The house is an adobe style, a one-story situation. Curtains cover the window next to the front door, and there isn't a single car parked anywhere. A giant metal tank with a hose stuck in it sits to the left of the house, and there's a single metal chair on the front porch, painted green. A tiny, circular ashtray rests at the leg of the chair, full of cigarettes and dirt, like it hasn't been used in a while.

What do I do? Do I knock? Do I leave the box right here? This part isn't clear. I'm seventy-five thousand dollars richer, but I don't know where to put the damn thing. I step up onto the porch and put my ear to the door. I listen, hoping someone's here, so the box doesn't end up in the wrong hands. I hear nothing, just the sound of emptiness on the other side. The wind blows against the side of the house, knocking rocks into the metal tub out front with the hose hanging out of it.

I place the box in the seat of the chair, as good a place as any, and start to walk back to the truck, when I stop. I look back at it. If I'm gonna know what's inside, now's my chance. I can find a way to seal it back up after I take a quick look. But, if I do that, will it make things worse? Would they know? What would happen to my brother? As I turn back to the house, about to make my way over to the box, I see a face peering at me from a tiny slit in the curtains. It's just a half-face, a single glaring eye, unblinking and directed right at me from behind the glass. I freeze. I wait for the face to move, for something to happen. My stomach becomes a cold cave going all the way into my legs. That eye, the way it looks at me, the way the half-face just stares, curtains frozen, as if hands gripped them on the other side. I back up, turn slowly, and head to the truck, all while feeling the face on my back. I get up into the cabin and back out, heading through the gate advertising WHEELER RANCH, and pull onto the main roads. Back in town, the pharmacy is dark, and the roads are just as empty as before. A dog runs up the sidewalk on my right, chasing an empty cup.

•

I get some gas before I leave town, some food for the road. I don't have to rush, but I'm nervous about the truck. It's probably been reported by now. I have to ditch it at some point, find something else. I get to the highway by late afternoon, but the sun's still strong. Five hours later, I'm back across the border into Arizona. A shaky sense of dread rolls up from my gut. But I ignore it. The desert seems blue, this time, instead of orange. It's the way the light hits it. The sky is getting dark, turning heavy. Stars prick the surface of it in little bright points. The bluffs look blue, too, as the road takes me further in, and I'm a few hours out from the turn-off, the one to Lukas's old farm house. I'm pretty sure I'm not far from it now, and I'm wondering what is really buried in that place. A lost suitcase full of cash. It's enough to push me onward, so I punch the gas a little harder. I've got some time to kill.

The radio plays nothing, just static, some voices. At

one point, there is a minute or so of Patsy Cline. I give up on the tunes and roll down the window. Lighting a cigarette, I keep my eye out for the turn-off. Occasionally, I look at the empty seat, and I think about him; who did I give a ride to? Where is Lukas now? I flip on my headlights when the desert goes fully black the way it does. The truck's beams slice along the dark road, flashing upon the torsos of cactuses, and once in a while, I feel like I'm waiting for someone to come up from behind the tall shapes. I remember the man's face, the worked, melancholic droop of his eyes; a man of hard-living, back there in that horror of a drive-in. I see Lukas running off behind the crumbling movie screen; I see him out there somewhere, still wandering in the desert, but somehow I know this is not true. I know none of this is true, and yet it is.

A darkened bluff flashes in my lights ahead. I think I recognize it, but I can't be sure. It comes up on the right. This is near the turn-off. I sit up, the muscles in my neck like corded wire, and sure enough, there's a road. It's right there, so I take it. The car leaps over a pothole, then corrects. I hear the same dirt and gravel hitting the underside of the truck, scattering to the fields on either side, and there's the barbed wire fence flashing in the high beams. The horizon glows a faint sliver far ahead. The rest of everything out here is nothing but black. The headlights make the road into a single line heading further into nothing. I'm looking to the left, trying to keep my eye out for the leaning house, its bent configuration, as if diving right into the dirt. But the land stays dark, and I only see interminable lines from the fences on either side going and going. A few minutes later, I'm at a small intersection. No stop sign, no signs at all, just a direction to choose. But I should see the house. I go forward, certain it's further up, but the land just extends itself.

The truck rides smooth despite the ruts, but it jerks, bounces hard to the right and the wheel snaps out of my fingers. The tire sinks into a pothole I don't see. The cabin tilts. Then the engine stalls after a few seconds. I get out quick and stumble around on weak legs. There in the shadows from the headlights I can see the tire bent outward, horizontal from the axel, half-in and half-out of a gaping pothole. How did I miss this? I kick the grill and shout a few more times before exhausting myself. Leaning against the truck, I smoke a cigarette, which tastes just like mud. I spit, crush the coal with my boot, then dig out what I can from the truck, including the blankets. I leave the keys in the ignition and start my trek down the side of the road in the same direction I was headed. The cold in the desert is sharp, so I wrap myself in one of the blankets and keep the other under my arm. I'm looking in all directions for the house but the stars out here are the only things I can see.

Half an hour later, maybe more, I'm at another intersection. I breathe in the cold air and look in all directions. I head west, thinking maybe I went down the wrong street to start with; that I'm over by a street or two. At a certain point, it's so quiet, its as though I can hear too much. Every small thing gets louder. I'm too aware of the sound of my own boots; this is the kind of awareness you get when you know you're not alone. I can feel someone there, someone right behind me, watching, like they've been here the whole time, just watching me go in circles, stumbling down this road in the dark. I stop and listen. More wind and rattling wire fences. I keep on and the feeling goes away, but not completely. When I reach the next intersection, I have a choice to go in the same direction, head east, or go back the way I came. I choose east, and it takes me further out. I'm so cold I have to keep my head down with both blankets over my head, like a hood. My legs and shoulders shake deep. My lungs go raw and my mouth carries the taste of blood in it. I'm hungry, and I want to lay down, just to sleep.

After a while, there aren't anymore intersections, just more road, and eventually the fences are gone, too, and I'm just walking in a field, but I don't know what I'm walking toward. It just keeps going and going, and I'm so cold that I don't care anymore. But the house is somewhere, I know it is. That's when I think I see a figure way ahead, just standing out there watching me in the dark. White movement, like a passing light. I can just make out a pair of shoulders, the surface of a face, a smear of features, a voice, something that says, *Come find me, I'm here, come find me here, I'm here, I'm right here,* just like that, and then nothing, because how could anything be here but me. It's just me, I know that. This is what I want to believe. But I follow it anyway because it moves like a flame, a tall flame cutting the dark. And when it's gone, I see the flutter of street lights, a city or a town maybe, just a few miles off. I could get there. I could make it. So I begin.

EXCAVATION

I won the Gorgon's head in a Bad Santa raffle. No one wanted it because no one knew what to do with it, or how to use it. More importantly, they were scared of it. It never worked the way they wanted it to. Most of the time, it did what it wanted; it was, after all, still a living head. I thought of it like a pet. But a pet that didn't really do much. I kept it where I lived. It was stored under an embroidered purple quilt with books stacked on top of it, and a large section of translucent-yellow citrine quartz on top of that. It looked like a bowling ball was under there, except that the snakes continually pushed against the quilt, looking for a way out, I suppose. Otherwise, it was quiet and it made for a great table.

•

I was born during the Great Pandemic in the early part of the century, which I heard about endlessly from my mother. Growing up seemed pretty average for a while, or normal. My mother had PTSD; watching my father aspirate in front of her during the tail end of his illness with the Great Virus diminished her. She never dated again, and masks often sent her into anxiety attacks if she ever saw one just laying around somewhere. She spent time in a mental hospital after a person spit in her face at a Target about a week after my dad was buried. This was because my mom chose to wear a mask in public. I got to the age of eight without any kind of virus taking over the world again, but it felt like growing up in the scattered remains of hurricane most of the time.

•

We got a decade of peace before the next big thing happened. That was about it, if you could call it "peace." It was another virus. And it was much worse, of course, and it killed millions more. Masks didn't work against this one because it could get in through any exposed part of your body, even a hair follicle, but my mother said it was funny how there was no longer an argument about wearing one, especially when people started watching their friends and families literally "unfold" right in front of them because that's what it was; it was like seeing overripe fruit split, burst, pop, and the skin slide right off the meat and everything comes tumbling out. Front yards full of innards, piles of organs around skeletons in sagging flesh. My mom laughed in the car once, a bit maniacally, like she was losing it as she drove me to school one day. Schools refused to close, and she laughed at that, too. "Just like fuckin' 2020! Things never fuckin' change!" But things did change once teachers started unfolding in front of students, leaving big, wet messes in the halls of schools. "What's wrong?" My mother spoke to no one in particular while steering us down a rain-slicked road one afternoon. "Not so concerned about your fucking freedom now, are you? You dumb mother-fuckers!"

I think she still harbored a lot of anger about what happened to my father, and the way she was treated back then. She wanted me to have more in the world than what we'd been given, but there was only so much she could do, or any of us, for that matter. The last day she came home from work (businesses remained open despite the virus because, well, money; people still put that before safety, and human or animal life, even then. Although we never really had money again), she had a thick line of blood running from her scalp to her jaw. The skin at the top of her skull was starting to peel away. She told me not come out of my room, or to come near her. I did what she asked, and I regretted it. It would have been nice to say goodbye, face-to-face.

•

Things that happened once the virus went away: basic electricity shut down in about 85 % of the world and most power grids collapsed, irrevocably. We returned to candles, fires, and some pre-Virus tech that didn't last very long, honestly. The soil went bad. Trite, I know, but how else to put it? So people no longer ate anything that grew; everything was manufactured, and it had to be picked up when it was made in your Slot, which was what everyone lived in. It was basically a neighborhood that got ransacked and emptied out. Or it was like mine, which was a neighborhood that never got finished back when people built them. All of the houses were just hollow wooden structures. The basic idea of a house was there, standing up in boards with its cement foundation, but there were no walls or insulation. There were partial walls in some. The houses that did get "finished" didn't really have windows or other things to block out the cold or the rain. We occupied incomplete homes; places that were perpetually stuck in a phase of possibility, but never moving forward. Yet we all got our own "house" at least. Mine was two stories. I could go up the steps and sit on wooden floors with my feet dangling out of the place where a window would be. I would watch the sun fall behind the clouds, which was a lot like watching a torch sink behind two thousand layers of cheesecloth. We never saw the sun again, to be frank. The weather changed to permanent cloud cover, rain, drizzle and cold, and it just stayed that way. Really old residents could be found limping around sometimes shouting about propaganda; they believed their brains had been messed with by an unseen entity to see a false sky; that, really, the sun was still shining—it was just someone else's fault that they couldn't see it. Once the power grids failed, and the general collapse of everything else happened, money became as good as seashells for bartering. Class systems dissolved pretty rapidly for the most part, and everyone lived wherever they could. It wasn't

Mad Max or anything, but it was our world just the way we made it.

•

I kept finding and collecting books from the last century; it was almost like they'd wished this type of existence into being with their stories. There were so many of these kinds of novels and most of them were about people trying to control other people, or trying to force people to live in a way that was fraudulent. Extremism ruled these fictitious lands: the most fascinating thing for minds of the late twentieth century. The early part of this century has some of that, too. Characters were often driven by unquestioned religious beliefs or obsessions, and there was never a limit to their absurdities. The novels were also about fear. Abuse of power is at the core of this, especially over such issues as rampant technology and science. It was like a suitcase of monsters that never got sorted properly. Writers appeared to create these stories in order to explain behavior or, in many cases, to place blame. It wasn't always clear, and I couldn't have said if any of it was very effective. If I could go back in time to tell these writers what it was really like, I'd explain that their stories left much to be desired when compared with the real shit; that we can never really imagine a worse hell for ourselves than the one that arrives unsuspected. I would tell them that real dystopias are banal; that it's just the leftovers of humanity struggling to survive in a sloppy fallout, woo-hoo. And humanity really speaks for itself, don't you think? These writers either gave people too much credit for massive amounts of destruction or risky superlatives for heaps of altruism, whichever pulled the most focus in these sensational stories.

If writers understood that our world actually became *this* simply through sheer arrogance, it's a lot less ridiculous than what they conjured for their books, which are at best more comforting than anything else. The biggest fiction might be altruism, however. Haven't seen much of that. Our world collapsed because everyone became a martyr overnight, which will do quite a bit of damage. You just don't see it until later. Ideology was more important than staying alive. No one respected anyone anymore, either; boundaries stopped mattering early on. It really was that simple. The right conditions were all there; it just required a creature that thought it was invincible, and there you have it. People are awesome.

•

So the thing was, when everything "ended" weird shit started happening. For example, a lot of supernatural and demonic shit in the old texts, but not in the way it was written. Some of us were better equipped to deal with it. Others just turned away and never acknowledged what was happening. This was how the Gorgon was found. A few miles from my Slot was an old lake that collapsed into a massive sinkhole. It was so big and dark, it was more of an abyss, just like I read about in books. People often flung themselves into it when they'd had enough and were ready to die, but all I could think was what if you never hit bottom—what if you just fell forever? It always gave me shivers to look at it, to imagine those who actually went through with leaping. Surrounding the abyss was a swamp with little mud islands, places you could sink into and drown. When one of these islands slid away, like a wet sleeve, and a giant snake-body with a human torso attached to it pushed to the surface, shit hit the fan on a macro-scale. It had thick, living snakes writhing on its head, each pushing in the mud. Everyone's hope for a return to a "Better Normal" vanished at the sight of that demonic weave.

•

The Gorgon had been dead for some time, obviously, and the story was clearly wrong since she still had her head. Perseus's heroism was evidently bullshit. Its lifeless snake-body—more like the size of a small whale with gray-green scales—had remained preserved, and the only thing that was living was the head, but not really "living," just functioning as it was supposed to, like a car alarm that kept going off, even though the car is totaled. A Man's Man from one of the male-centered parts of the Slot wanted to show his strength by getting in there and checking to make sure it was truly dead, so he poked it with a stick. Then he stood with his hands on his hips, shaking his head, like how silly that this group was so totally terrified by such a dumb, dead, mythical creature lying hidden here all these endless millennia.

He turned its head to the side so he could take a good look at its face. This was when its eyes opened and the snakes went ape-shit. The guy just staggered, hunched over, and made a sound like he was about to crap all over himself. Then he went right to stone. One of the snakes lurched out and bit his foot for good measure, but it only made him unsteady. He fell backwards, a gray statue, and rolled to the edge of the gaping chasm, then dropped right in. The alien looking snakes coiled and hissed, and everyone ran.

•

Eventually a team of people found a way to sever the head from the corpse and put it into a potato bag. They kicked the lifeless snake/human body-combo into the abyss with the other stone statues of people who attempted to chop off its head. A man in makeshift overalls and a bib, who also wore mismatched cowboy boots, shouted to the crowd watching in anticipation a few yards back in the swamp: "This here's fuckin' Medusa! Jesus, I'll be…It's the fuckin' Medusa head! Look at them snakes!" Then he belched, followed by the longest, strangest fart before handing over the potato bag to a helpless looking woman in a purple muumuu.

•

The Gorgon's head quickly became trouble. First it was a high-ticket item. Only those who could afford to barter for it, got it. It was like owning something rare found in a cave somewhere, although its value was always a mystery. At first, people seemed fascinated by it, like a gun is fascinating to a child. They pointed it at things, turning rodents and wildlife into little statues and then went around selling them at the Slo-market in the center of our Slot. People were disturbed, so they refused to buy the little figurines of mutated squirrels caught in an act of final scavenging. The confused terror in its tiny eyes while awkwardly clutching a nut was a turn off. When that failed, the head got traded again, and it started to lose its mysterious value when people began using it on each other in moments of rage, or when kids accidentally turned themselves into stone. One woman, six months pregnant, made the mistake of facing the Gorgon, which turned her baby into a heavy stone fetus, rather than her. Anti-abortion groups protested her decision to have it removed (yes, they still existed, even in this time), so they attacked her, eventually killing her by stoning her to death in a cul-de-sac. In the spirit of human rage, the husband took the stone fetus from his dead wife's womb and hand-delivered it to the house of the anti-abortion group's leader with a note that said, "He's all yours. Please take care of him." But it was when people discovered that the Gorgon's head did more than turn living things into stone that the head finally lost all mystical value and ended up abandoned, or shuffled from place to place with no one who knew what to do with it, yet never making the decision to get rid of it for good. It was one thing for this snake-writhing head to turn your child to stone, but it was another for it to reveal a secret or to make a person aware of something they had worked hard to re-press. Left and right, men went crazy; it seemed, more and more, a man would accidentally peer right into the Gorgon's silvery eyes and suddenly start screaming in the middle of the street. While dropping to his knees, you would often hear a man scream: "I'm a cock lover! Holy God damn, I'm a cock lover! No! This can't be!"

The Man's Man section of the Slot (really just a private enclave for men who wanted to live together away from others and, as their slogan went, "Protect masculinity from the erosion of the world"), had publicly displayed a ban punishable by "severe torture" and who knows what else, if anyone was caught within a meter of their section carrying the Gorgon's head. The leader of this enclave would often be found in the Slo-market shouting in a corner about it, saying such things as: "It is an INJUSTICE to force a man to admit to loving men! It is an INJUSTICE to push a man's face into the mud of his own soul! If a man says he loves the opposite gender, we should believe him, even if it's not true! For this reason, the Gorgon's head should be destroyed!" He did not seem to understand what he said, or the looks he incurred in the saying of it.

But no matter how many men ended up exposed to their wives and children for being a "cock lover" after accidentally crossing paths with the severed Gorgon head, it still hung around. If it wasn't the ripping away of denial that the head engendered, it was confession after confession, or realization, like a stream of chants all over the neighborhood: "I'm a whore…I"m a bastard…I'm a murderer…I robbed my own sister…I butchered my brother with his own axe…I lie, and I enjoy it…I'm a sociopath…I beat and harm animals and children…I'm not better than others…I'm going to die one day…I'm dumb…"

If the horrors and onslaughts of everything humanity had been through wasn't enough to break it before now, this very well could. It seemed the destruction of humanity was not in outside events, like viruses or natural disasters, but in being forced to admit to itself what it really was; the Gorgon revealed—in a rather short time—that the destruction of humanity was a process of people coming out of denial. It seemed that if you took away man's ability to lie to himself about who and what he actually was, you sewed the seeds for apocalypse. The Gorgon's head brought awareness to everyone in one fashion or another, and that was just too much for people to handle.

So it made its way to me.

The Bad Santa raffle was a holdover from decades prior. It had evolved from a humorous game performed in kindness into a royal battle built upon punishment and shame. What a person won't do for some company once in a while.

•

I never looked at the Gorgon directly, of course. For obvious reasons, I didn't want to die being turned into a statue, but I was far from afraid of discovering I was a "cock lover," because I was one. I have always been quite clear on that. Unfortunately, dating still sucked. The dissolution of boundaries between people really went away sometime in the early twenty-first century with "social media," (there were stories about it, but no one had phones anymore, or computers, or anything— we sent letters and wrote notes. Older people called this "barbaric"). I heard many of the older guys talk about "apps" where you could order someone to your house like food and soullessly fuck them all night. This was performed over and over again without thought, they said. People would wake up to messages that were only pictures, some displaying a man's raw, used asshole, or a hard, dripping penis, and these were meant to entice you to desire them. The older guys said it was a really great time in history. With or without the apps, this still happened in a manner of speaking. My walls were clear tarps nailed to boards making up the general structure of my house. Some of the tarps got loose and fluttered around, ghostlike, and made rippling sounds.

Anyone could come in through these "walls" because there weren't any visible ones. You hoped people would knock on a board, or tap on a tarp, say hello, something, but many didn't. They just walked right in. This happened with dating often. If word got around that you were looking for a companion, many visitors arrived in a night, or day, whichever it was didn't really matter. But it was always kind of a downer when you woke up in the morning to find a completely naked man bent over right in front of you, his puckered anus in your direct line of vision. It took a lot of patience. But, eventually, after a long exhausted sigh, I got them to leave. They usually responded with something like, "You seem cool. We should hang out." This said while peering at me between their legs over a drooping, welt-covered scrotum. They slid out of one of the open tarps, incredulous that their advances just didn't work. Since this constituted dating, I stayed single. As an added precaution, I uncovered the Gorgon's head and aimed her gaze in the direction most guys were likely to enter my house. I got more sleep this way.

•

"People are dumb as fuck, don't forget that. And worse, they like being dumb." My mother would tell me this while buying me something, like frozen yogurt or cookies. It would come from nowhere, seemingly, and with no context, but now that I was older and on my own, I understood what she meant, especially when I hiked to the Slots a few miles down the road from ours. There was one I went to often. It had huge black gates, and the houses were gigantic castles, or looked like castles. If it was one thing the dystopian books got right, it was the whole abandonment angle. I mean, every single house looked completely frozen as if the house itself was in motion at one time, then everything settled at once. Boxes, clothes, appliances, food, trinkets, left anywhere and everywhere, all suddenly meaningless.

Sometimes there were black stains on floors, stairs,

and bathtubs where people unfolded. I always stayed away from them. One time, I found two skeletons. It looked like a mother and her little girl (the clothes from those times gave it away), and the mother appeared to be making a choice between something unseen and her daughter, before both of them died. I couldn't tell what the choice was, but I decided it didn't matter; it was obvious from the way their corpses were arranged that this little girl was far less important than whatever her mother reached for across the room. It's hard not to see this decision as stupid, even if you don't know what was happening at the time, like most of history.

•

On a page from a book torn in half, laying in the rubble of a burned-out house, a blue hardback—*Civilization and the Manufacture of Quarries,* by Dr. Joseph Stripe: *And what of the things that unearth us? Isn't it that which we keep burying that eventually rises to the surface again and again until we're forced to look at it, lest it destroy us all? We are, after all, so masterful at the act of internment. Epistemology, along with some record of events, a continuum, if you will, has...*

From a guide for hiking through high altitudes:

...it is recommended that you dispense with the unnecessary; every extra pound is a hindrance. Your goal is to protect your ability to move lightly through tough spaces. Everything else can be ignored. Ask yourself, do I really need this object? Can I travel lightly without it? Remember, the environment around you doesn't care that you are there; you're the only one that notices it. It does not notice you, and it will consume you in any manner possible. Thousands of people disappear on mountains every year. Thousands more never reach their desired location, but instead perish where they stop. Often it is too costly to carry or air-lift the bodies down, so there they stay, forever between where they began and where they were headed...

I took both of them with me.

•

Many of the enclaves in my Slot catered to those who were around before The End. One house was dedicated to people who missed phones; they sat around with props of them, painted on boards, paper, or even stones, whatever they could find, and pretended to "text" people, or to "swipe"; they did this for hours, and if you went inside, none of them would look up at you or say anything, which was part of the experience. You felt, momentarily, like you did't exist, and that made them feel good—it was the whole point, apparently. Some even threw their "phones" in forced anger over a "text" that showed up, or a "meme," whatever that was. Some would shake and clutch their chests, pacing the room because their "battery was about to die!" Then they pretended to "plug it in," and sighed heavily because they were afraid they might miss another "text," or a "status update."

The last guy to take me on a date thought this would be fun for us both. He stamped around and demonstrated numerous strange poses, like a plant with diarrhea, and then said, "Okay, now rate me!"

"Rate you?"

"Yeah, 'like' me for my poses."

"How do I—?"

"Just click: 'like!'"

He grabbed my hand and pulled it into the air in front of me, extended my finger, and made me 'press' an imaginary button. Then he bounced around, and said, gleefully, "See, now I have even more likes! Okay, now *subscribe* to me!"

•

Night was my favorite time in the Slot. The whole place usually went completely quiet, except for dogs barking far away. Little trails of smoke rose from different parts of houses into the sky. Sometimes you could see the orange flicker of candles along the streets, or in dirty windows, from my empty second floor. We didn't see anything at night except the moon through sheets of clouds, but sometimes it was bright enough to show the tips of trees in the mountains a few miles away. Sometimes it even looked like a completely different place. I once thought I saw a star.

•

I decided to go to a different Slot five miles away that I had not been to, but noticed once on one of my treks. With the Gorgon's head in the sling on my back, and my other pack over my left shoulder, I headed off early to see what I could find. The wind blew over me, hard and cold, and the drizzle was worse than usual, close to the feeling of constantly being spit on. Lowering my head seemed to help. I passed the Re-Civilization camp where people went when they wanted to learn how to be "civilized" again. Some called it empathy training. Apparently, in the early part of the century, sociopathy was on the rise and was often encouraged, along with anti-intellectualism. The tops of their tents were visible from the road. I knew a guy who completed the entire stay once. He said he had no idea how to look at someone until he went in there, which was something else you learned. I heard people received training on how to interpret social cues, such as how to look each other in the eyes and there was even a whole month spent on manners. Becoming literate and how to assert boundaries were some of the other trainings. Some people didn't make it all the way, though, and we heard those stories, too. They ended up forming their own offshoot communities called "Freedom Camps," which did the opposite of the civilizing ones. You just had to go a few miles in the other direction and the earth was still flat.

Schools also failed for the most part, which might be why the camps were started. There were some who tried to reinstate the old way of doing things, but it just didn't work. Any time someone felt challenged by a teacher, or a parent disagreed with a grade, and the student had to think critically about anything, they handcuffed the teacher in the night and tossed them into the sinkhole. Then they found another teacher who would agree with them and give them the grades they wanted; there was even a signed pact that no teacher could challenge students. But the minute this changed, off went the teacher into the abyss. Almost any problem you can think of was solved using the abyss; in fact, things were rarely discussed or worked through. Finally they couldn't find anyone who was willing to take the post any longer. But no one cared. Or, even more accurate, no would-be instructors felt like it was worth risking a fate in the chasm, so they closed up the schools, and then, later on, someone burned them down. Everyone got schooled however they could after that. Most were illiterate, which was always a source of contention at the Slo-market. The pressure was too much for some, so they usually left for the Freedom Camps where they didn't have to think about it.

Up on the left, I spotted the new Slot I wanted to explore. This one had higher fences and the houses had about four chimneys per roof. Many had the same gray tile and were painted the same beige color. I flung my rope across the metal spikes at the top, then climbed up and over, dropping into a garden full of soft mulch and thorny trees. I faced a street of houses that probably cost within the millions, Pre-Recent Virus. The look of things was standard apocalypse aesthetic: cars overturned, black smears where bodies unfolded in the street, burn marks up the sides of houses, trash everywhere, broken windows. You get the idea.

Up on the far left of the street was a house with four red chimneys. It stood out from the rest, so I decided to start there. Parked in the driveway was a silver Mercedes with dissolved, black piles of innards where people had once tried to get away before it was too late. A bumper sticker on the back read: "Ban the mask! Don't tread on my freedom! I'm free to breathe however I want to!" It had a picture of a person's face with an expression of deep breathing with a placid grin. I looked at the piles of black goop all over the seats and decided there was nothing in the car worth taking.

The front door was shut, but it opened like most of them do. Locks and attempts at boarding up any kind of shelter went away once people realized if someone wanted inside, they were going to find a way; and with no law enforcement, justice system, or enough of anything to stop them, people just gave up. Once inside, the place appeared mostly untouched. Stairs faced the entrance. The carpet was white and the foyer had blue tile. The living room to the right had a white couch and a massive wooden coffee table covered with thick, wide art books. Some were open as if they had been flipped through recently. Near the windows looking on the front yard was a baby grand piano, its bench pushed back against the bookshelf making up the wall behind it. The bookshelf had a ton of hardbacks held up by golden peacock bookends. I opened my pack and began shoving them inside. The shelf on the left had some more. I took some of those, too.

The head in the sling on my back grew restless. The snakes twitched around, sniffing at my shoulders and coiling against my spine. I took it off for a moment and leaned it against the coffee table along with my pack. I grabbed the bench and sat at the piano. I hadn't seen a piano in years, even forgot what they sounded like. I was hesitant to touch the keys for some reason, but when I did, the tuning wasn't so bad. I played around on them for a minute, making up songs, and then I just kept doing it until almost an hour passed. I felt a strange kind of calm afterwards. Even the snakes had stopped fidgeting and were silent. Standing on the stairs watching me, I noticed, was slender guy in white pants and a pink shirt. He had dark hair, and he stared right at me.

"I'm sorry," I said, standing up, "I didn't realize anyone had this house. I thought it was abandoned like the others."

"You are fine. Don't worry. Just recently took this one."

"Okay, well, I apologize. I'll leave now."

"Please, stay. I really liked your playing."

"I don't know that I'd call it genuine playing."

"Well, it is something. I loved hearing it. Even if it was made up."

"Thank you."

"Please," he said, and gestured at the couch. "Have a seat. We have nothing to offer by way of food or water, but some company would be nice."

I instinctually went for my bags and almost headed to the door, but the guy smiled at me, and he was so attractive, it was difficult to say no. So I joined him on the couch, and he asked me if I liked art. We flipped through some of the books together, and talked about which ones he thought were the best, and which were not. He sat with confidence, and he looked awfully clean, considering the state of things. Watching him, I almost felt as though we'd been transported away from now, to a time far gone and beyond resurrection. He held his muscular arms stretched along the top of the couch. His smooth skin was olive-colored.

He smiled at me again.

"It's been a while for you, hasn't it?" he said.

"I'm not sure what you mean."

"Hanging out with people, or going on a date."

"A date? I mean, well, I don't…"

"It's fine. These are challenging times."

I just nodded and folded my arms across my chest.

"You should relax," he said. "I'm Alan."

He laughed and turned to face me. "I had actually been thinking the other day how magical it would be if a cute guy just showed up in my living room. And here you are."

"I guess so."

"I'm sorry if I'm so direct. I guess I'm tired, too. And I also want a companion in all of this. We could at least be friends, right? Maybe more…"

"A friend would be nice," I told him.

He took my hand in his.

"Me too," he said.

He leaned forward, kissed me right under my eye, and told me he'd be back.

I stayed on the couch while he went upstairs. My hands were slick and my stomach felt warm. I flipped through some more of the art books with numb fingers. When he returned, he had another guy with him. This one was older. He wore black pants and a white shirt, and looked oddly clean as well. He smiled down at me with an expression of approval.

Nodding, the older guy said, "Perfect."

"What's going on?" I asked.

Alan looked at me, and in a soft voice, he said, "This is my husband."

"Your *husband*? Oh. I thought you were here alone."

"Ha, no no. We're here with our adopted daughter, Brilliance. She's playing in the kitchen right now. You just can't hear her."

"I'm so sorry. I'm even more embarrassed to be here."

"Don't be. My husband and I have been looking for a third, and you dropped in at the right time."

"A third?"

Alan and his husband looked at each other, and laughed.

"Well, yeah. Sometimes we like to spice up *our* existence."

"If only we could get a fourth, or even a fifth," said Alan's husband, suddenly morose, as if they'd tried to get pregnant multiple times, and it just wasn't working.

"Let's not look a gift horse in the mouth, honey," said Alan, lightly spanking his husband.

"Are you a top or a bottom? Also, how big are you?"

"I've gotta go," I said, and reached for my bags. The Gorgon's head sprang to life in the sling as if irritated. It reminded me of a spoiled cat.

"Ooh, what's that?" said Alan, who took it upon himself to lift the head right out of the sling and hold it up. I caught a glimpse of the side of it, but made sure not to look. The dark snakes rose up all at once. They contorted, angry as if being woken unnecessarily; several wet mouths gaped, fangs exposed. Giant clear hooks wedged into shining black gums. The jaw of the Gorgon opened a little. A gray tongue slid out, its wet surface catching the murky light from the window. Alan's face drained, his eyes wide, and his husband bolted back upstairs. When he dropped the Gorgon's head, it rolled under the piano. I had to paw around until I found it. The snakes never did anything; they knew me. I pulled it forward and draped the bag over it without looking, just like I always do. Alan dropped to his knees, clutching his face and screaming gutturally at the room.

"I'm a piece of shit!" he shouted, tears pouring down his face. "Ohh God, I'm a fucking piece of shit! Nothing is ever good enough for me. I want to have my cake and eat it, too. I never wanted a daughter. I did it to keep my husband around, but only because he has a big dick, and that's all I care about. I'm a fucking pice of shit! Oh God, I'm horrible. I've thought of leaving them both just because I'm sick of sharing food with that stupid bitch. I made my husband kill the squatters that had this place before us because I wanted white carpet and a baby grand. I'm shallow. I have no intellect. I'm hateful. I'm fake. I hate *myself*. I only feel an *idea* of love when I'm fucking. *Fucking* is how I feel alive. Otherwise, I'm a shallow nothing. I don't know what love is or how to love. I'm human garbage, and I use people to get what I want because I'm a piece-of-shit-parasite. Before all this happened, I poisoned my best friend and put her into a coma because she deleted me from social media, and I lost subscribers from her posts. I stole money from my mother. I have a rape fantasy involving a broomstick."

Then he stopped, an abrupt halt, like someone who had been vomiting and their stomach had nothing left.

This was what the Gorgon did.

"What is that thing?" he panted, sweat pouring down his face. His pallor was greasy and slick. Tears dripped from his chin.

"It's the head of a Gorgon. Medusa. A mythical creature we found buried in a mud mound next to an abyss in my Slot five miles that way."

He stared at me, incredulous.

"Why did it do that?"

I shrugged. "In the old stories it says it's just supposed to turn people to stone. But I guess it does other things someone failed to mention. Or, maybe this is just another form of that. You do look quite petrified, if I say so myself."

Alan nodded, drool falling.

"Get out," he muttered.

"Already ahead of you," I smiled at him, hoping he would get the joke, but he just glared, the drool still coming.

Outside, the cool air felt better. I took my new finds and started the trek home.

●

That night, after flipping through some of my older books about dystopias and the end of the world, I thought I would write my own—a dystopia of a dystopia, perhaps. What would that look like? I sat upstairs in my usual spot, watching the rain collect in the streets. Warm, orange candle flickers appeared in some of the windows, and the same dogs barked. The tarps around me fluttered in small gusts pushing through the invisible walls of the second floor.

What I got down wasn't much, but it was something. I had to start somewhere, even if it didn't matter, or no one would see it. At the very least, I had to do that:

In this universe, the old gods stay unburied. Here, people know how to love. Everything starts in a small, mostly quiet village in the middle of nowhere with not much of a sun, or even a moon, and definitely no stars. It begins, no matter how impossibly, with a friend—the most unusual thing in the world.

EVIDENCE OF VISIBILITY FROM SPACE

The first thing I remember is the tile of their bathroom floor, which formed a clear, sprawling swastika pattern in sea green and pale blue. They must have spent a month alone deciding how the bathroom should look, and it was only much later that I decided it couldn't have been done for the purposes of abusing irony in some way. Leena and Julian were educated enough to know better. But it kept me wondering how it got there, how either of them would allow such an oversight. Was it an accident? They weren't the kind of couple you associated with recklessness, myopia, or narcissism. When I met them, their relationship conveyed the exact opposite: cozy benevolence, an otherworldly welcoming. Their home was a cultural orphanage. It asserted the same aura of benevolence while also communicating that it somehow knew better; as a space it granted all of the shoddily made pin sculptures and handmade twig-and-paper ornaments a chance among the other, more substantial works showcased in odd corners with intentional messiness.

I learned about them from Jackie, who'd introduced us when Leena came to town for her mother's funeral. I met Leena first. When she came to me after a long hug from Jackie where we all stood waiting for a table in the stringently named "Arts District," I thought only of the word *wan*, and then *pale*, and then *stick-like*. But she was refined and, after she embraced me, said how Jackie had found a brother in me, and whispered that she had waited long enough for us to meet. I understood how it all worked for her. To be anything other than *stick-like* would undermine her, take away. I saw Julian before I met him. He stood at a distance from us, behind Leena and Jackie. His eyes reminded me of soaked corkwood. They were curious and searched everything. Julian had a bit too much visible curiosity. His slicked hair and jeans tucked into clean, unblemished Gore-Tex boots emphasized this, and left him somewhat helpless in his attempt to hide it.

When our table was ready, the waiter led us to a corner on the edge of the courtyard. A blue-tiled fountain trickled to our left in a shadowed garden, splashing down the stuccoed wall of the restaurant. Behind the hills, and the houses going up and down them like an uneven spine, clouds sat, foam-thick and gray. A cold wind blew up the street and across our table ruffling napkins and knocking cardboard coasters to the ground.

"Spring is really taking hold," said Leena. Her knotted scarf sat piled around her neck in dense loops of expensive wool. Her fingers, covered in jagged silver and turquoise, pulled tentatively at the front of it. Julian sat to my right with his legs stretched forward and boots out, as if waiting for someone, anyone, to say something about them.

"It's amazing we got out," said Julian. "Every time we leave Leena's afraid the house is burning down."

She looked toward the hills and the homes, the larger clouds.

"I'm not that bad," she said, dropping her hand to her lap.

"Leena and Julian are moving here in a month, right guys?" said Jackie.

"Something like that," said Julian. He leaned forward and grabbed his glass of water. He crunched the ice, lips held back.

When I asked the reason for the move, Leena turned in her chair so that she faced the road, then mentioned her mother and the rest of her family.

"They can't handle it," she said. Her mother had hung herself in the garage while a Brenda Lee song played on repeat. "They're disjointed. Everything's disjointed."

"But there's good news, too," said Jackie.

"Julian is editing a new collection that's going to be published by Phaidon."

"That's great news," I said.

"And the photographer is here. So it all works out."

"I never want you guys to leave," said Jackie. She leaned over and took Leena's arm, squeezed it and placed her head on Leena's shoulder. Jackie's red lips caught the sun, and her white skin seemed whiter. Blue plastic bracelets clacked over her prominent wrist bones.

"You guys should come to our place after this," said Julian.

"Yes, you have to," said Leena.

"Where are you staying?" I asked.

"Our new house," said Julian, as if I should know this by now. His black hair, I noted, was pulled into a tiny ponytail at the back of his head; a red rubber band held it.

"It just isn't finished yet," he said.

"Only one more month," said Leena.

Every weekend, the summer was spent at their house, which remained unfinished, but they seemed to want it that way. People came and went from Friday night until early Monday morning. The backyard chiminea reeked of newspaper and pinion wood. The sofa in the living room soon became a bed for Jackie and me when we were full of the wine Julian brandished from what he referred to as their "quaint cellar." He left two or three times a night, if the stores were open, returning with new cheeses and uncured meats. While he cooked for us, sometimes a third or fourth dish around 5:00 AM, he told us in causual tones about his volunteer work; he'd studied sign language so he could help deaf children learn to read; he bought coffee for the same homeless man downtown every day (free-trade and organic, of course); he voted in every election and kept all of the stickers declaring: "I VOTED!"; he performed in the bi-monthly puppet show for children in the cancer center of the hospital; he helped with re-cycling and created a neighborhood compost pile; he donated blood every six months; and, when the weather became cruel, he shoveled the snow from his neighbors' driveways.

Leena didn't work. She spent her time making wooden homes for the two turtles they had jointly owned for the last fifteen years. She made glass ornaments and arranged to use a friend's kiln for her earthen tableware collection, which was sold in full sets every month at a small gallery in the Arts District and was later picked up by West Elm.

"It's just West Elm," she said once while eating a blackberry dipped in cream, whipped only moments before by Julian in the kitchen.

"Yeah," said Julian. "But it's not the Arts District."

"He just says that because he wants me to promote it."

"You *should* be promoting it. It's not like you self-produced an album."

"One of our friends," whispered Leena. "One of them *self-produced.* I mean it *looks* like a real album anyway."

Jackie asked her who it was. When I realized I knew the album, I told them I had no idea the musician had done it alone, but that the album stood out.

"There's that stigma," said Julian. "A quality factor."

"Isn't that pretty much a dated idea at this point?" I suggested.

"I don't know," said Leena, snorting. "Is it art if it's not hanging in a gallery?"

"I think it's an *approval* thing," said Jackie. "Systems and institutions of *approval*. Does it really matter? Surely you'd support it if it was the same album, but went through a record company, or something, right?"

"That depends on the reviews," said Julian, ordering us to the kitchen bar for his organic, stuffed mushrooms he had handpicked from the garden out back.

"You guys," mumbled Jackie through a mouthful of Julian's work. "What are you going to do with this place? I know it's still in progress, but the lighting outside…"

"Is money well-spent. It's meant to give a warm look, like it's warm in here, you know?" responded Leena.

"Have your neighbors said anything? I wonder how it looks to them."

Leena shrugged and pushed her bowl of Julian's mushrooms aside, uneaten.

"They see us, that's all that matters," she said.

"The other houses around here seem so dark by comparison, like little shells but…"

"That doesn't happen to houses like ours," said Leena with a form of confidence that left the room quiet for a while.

"I'm going to sleep," she said. "Goodnight everyone."

We said goodnight to her as she turned the corner and disappeared down the hallway with her mauve robe trailing on the tiles.

When August hit, Julian started complaining about Leena to me in secret. He came to my house alone, unannounced mostly, and often with wine and sacks full of food. He described my house as "suitable." His conversations hinged on authenticity; nothing was authentic anymore, not even Leena. He was starved for the level of attention he "deserved" and spoke of the vanilla, lackluster "punishment" he called the sex he shared with his wife. Every possible fracture was magnified.

"Don't I do enough?" he cried. "She's got me by the balls, but doesn't do anything with them. She's become so…I don't know, *frail*. Frankly, it's revolting."

This continued through September when the weather changed, and Saturdays were spent solely at my home, the same wine and cheeses and glazed plates cooked by him and presented on my dining room table. He did this with practiced modesty. Only once did I forget to congratulate him on his cooking finesse. Apologizing for it later, he stopped me, and said, "Leena knows you appreciate it. That's all that matters."

"I've got to show you something," he said one evening. He handed me a collection of Bergman films.

"A friend of mine sent these to me. A new print. They won't be released until next year. They're incredible. Have you seen *Through A Glass Darkly*?"

I admitted that I hadn't, so we watched it, drinking down the rest of the wine. Julian finished a bottle on his own, shouting at the screen, with his hands near his face, that real film was dead and where was David Lynch in all of this? I didn't have an answer for him. I told him to stay on the sofa if he needed to. I left him for the bathroom where I brushed my teeth. The mix of rich tannin and synthetic mint swam over my tongue. Drunkenly, I fell on my bed. I closed my eyes and drifted down, a sensation more from the wine than fatigue. Minutes later the bed shifted. Weight slid in beside me and a hot hand cupped my shoulder, rubbing it in tight, firm circles. I didn't move and, feigning sleep, waited for Julian to leave. I made my body into a form of rejection. *"You're all the same, aren't you?"* he whispered. *"Come on…"* He removed his pants and pressed himself into my thigh. I gripped the edge of the bed, ready to snap up and tell him to get out, now, when he stopped, rolled away, and left the room soon after. I heard the front door shut and my home was suddenly very quiet.

During the following week Jackie arranged a party, inviting more people than could fit in Julian and Leena's house. I knew about it from her. When I arrived I noticed Julian's agent and editor had guests of their own and spoke to Julian almost exclusively. Leena walked around barefoot holding a glass of Petrón and orange juice. Clusters of tea candles in Leena's earthenware cups lit corners of the entryway like burning eggs. It appeared random, but it wasn't. Paintings on the walls possessed a phosphorescent quality. Deep purples, reds, and turquoise cut across hand-stretched canvases shipped from Leena's home in Scotland. On speakers above us, the Wayne Shorter Quartet burst through conversations; a rush moved through everyone, jolted by the piano, and then a plying, tentative saxophone. I was introduced to the collective that made up the other artists of Leena's earthenware gallery. They stood together in a group, some sharing the same uniform of rolled-up jeans, torn sweaters, overalls and knitted caps. Leena retired on the brick patio near the chiminea sitting cross-legged; she pulled up grass from the yard behind her and tugged it apart with her fingers, nodding encouragingly at one of the other artists squatting in front of her. He spoke so earnestly it bordered on self-debasement. He gestured gently with his drink, forearms on his thighs, a long manicured beard under wayfarer glasses and a shaved head. Everyone at the party was drawn to Julian and Leena as if they were oracles. The guests were aware of their connections and wealth, something the couple worked so hard to diminish only so that in some way it became bigger than them: over a glass of water or an unnecessary compliment, prosciutto and olives arranged by Julian—*all* of it was met with humiliating honesty by the other guests as if it couldn't be accomplished by anyone else. Together, Leena and Julian were a magic couple, shedding and imparting fortune on all those who walked among them.

On the lawn, back near the Koi pond, was a small faction of guests attempting some form of spoken word performance accompanied by little howls of approval and support; the words of the speaker carried across various groups of chatter: "Fuck momma's sweet pussy! Fuck momma's sweet pussy! Get down get down get down get down..."

Leena patted me on the arm on the way to grab some photographs to show one of the other guests. She said hello and moved on. I saw it as a need to jump quickly between people more than an awareness of what her husband had done. I doubted he'd told her. What would it accomplish? Only that it might become currency Leena could use later if she wanted. Julian found me and offered some of his wine. It was mechanical on his part, but not unfriendly. I suppressed anything that might acknowledge his recent actions, and took the glass he offered. When he toasted, our glasses smacked, and I caught a tiny smug twist to his mouth, enough to know that underneath it was some subtle truth he hadn't meant to escape. I understood my invitation to the party, then, was not genuine.

Jackie's new date walked with her from group to group. He rolled his own cigarettes and shook hands with a deliberate, useless force. He digitized film footage for different movie companies and travelled with various crews to locations when he wanted to. "One of the perks!" he'd said. She told Leena and me about his tattoos: full sleeves and a partial chest piece. He also had an awkward circumcision job and, despite her many attempts, she confessed she just couldn't get used to it.

"We have such a great group, you know?" she said to both of us. "You, me, and Julian."

Julian stood off to the left on the grass talking to his editor.

"The house should have gravity," he said, indicating his roof. "We wanted it to have a certain *weight* to it. Some crucial importance."

I said nothing to Jackie about Julian, or our night. I said nothing to anyone. After Jackie's party, two months passed where neither myself, nor Jackie, heard from them. She said Julian spent most of his time with the photographer. Leena went to Scotland for two weeks to visit her father who had halted an excavation to nurse his rapidly encroaching cerebral palsy. Jackie didn't contact me again until after the New Year when, suddenly, she wanted to meet. Over the phone, her voice had an unfamiliar urgency. I joined her downtown at a sports bar of her choosing. On the table in front of her sat an untouched plastic basket full of onion rings. I reached for one and they were cold.

"It's just, I *love* Julian, you know? Julian can do no wrong. He's practically perfect," said Jackie.

The waiter brought her a glass of straight vodka with a maraschino cherry sliver stuck to the side. I wanted to point it out to her, but decided to let her keep talking.

"I don't understand why Leena would bother. Did she think I would say *yes*? I mean, an entire *month* with Mika. I don't know how she could ask that of me."

Mika, once one of Jackie's closest friends, went by two names, although she rarely asked to be referred to as Lexi, the one she made up for herself. Jackie explained this as her "Gemini nature." It was when Jackie chose to have her second abortion that Mika accompanied her in support. She'd sworn to Jackie, a pledge to keep the experience from Jackie's parents. Under the pretense of concern, Mika had staged an "emotional intervention," and without Jackie knowing, confessed not just the handholding and Jackie's depression, but also let Jackie's father know of the first abortion. Done as a sophomore at Vanderbilt, she'd only told Mika. Both of Jackie's parents subsequently abandoned her and retreated into a Southern-Baptist church community. Jackie was left without an income, and was subsequently forced out of Vanderbilt due to her dwindling bank account. Her parents had not spoken to her in three years.

Jackie continued, gesticulating wildly, saying that during Leena and Julian's New Year's party, they'd invited her with them to Europe for a month and then, with their standard, languid nonchalance, mentioned that Mika would also be going.

"Leena acted as if I *shouldn't* be bothered by this. Both of them know what she did, but still invited her.

Does that mean I should second-guess their integrity? What should I do? They *are* good people. They are *such good people!*"

Jackie registered the confused expression on my face when she mentioned the New Year's party.

"Oh, I meant to tell you. Didn't Leena call you? I mean, I can't *believe* no one said anything," she stammered, and then added, oddly: "Why weren't you there?"

I changed the subject, and asked what she planned to do about her invitation to Europe.

"Well, *Leena* said, 'Surely you can *ignore* her for a month and go with us anyway,' but I was incredulous and said *no*, of course."

Jackie finished her drink and made a point of stating that Leena and Julian were truly thoughtful people who rarely passed judgment and couldn't have meant any harm by their invitation. I said nothing to this; I paid for both of our drinks, and we left.

Leena, Mika, and Julian flew to Italy in March; Julian announced he would be spending two weeks with a single sculpture at the Bargello Gallery in Florence, and then Ghiberti's *Gates of Paradise.*

"Julian says it's the only way he could *really* experience it," Jackie reported. "You know, it's what you do with things like that."

Only Mika returned from the trip in June. Jackie and I met her at a bar where she told us of Julian's disappearance. All three of them had split up shortly after they'd arrived in San Marino, each seeking something different. No one had agreed on anything, according to Mika. Julian vanished somewhere in Nantes, and his contract with Phaidon was cancelled in April.

"Disappeared?" said Jackie, a hand pressed flat on her chest.

"We just lost track of him."

Mika told us that Leena had decided not to pursue an investigation.

"Leena didn't want to find him," she said. "And she jettisoned Italy for Scotland." Last she heard Leena had taken over her father's estate indefinitely. I presented the question of Julian's whereabouts again. Why weren't they concerned? Shouldn't someone try to go and look for him? Mika shrugged at the inquiry. I studied her. I sought some restricted knowledge in her face. Did she know anything? What did it matter if she did?

I wouldn't see Jackie again until a year later. She was coming out of a liquor store. She looked fuller and requested that we have lunch or dinner, or something.

The man with the tattoos was long gone, there was so much to say, please, will you? When she spoke, I negotiated the idea that things might be different had I given Julian what he wanted that night; had I broken the boundaries of friendship and helped him take revenge on his wife by getting him off, we might be at their house now, drinking Julian's wine and watching him cook veal. My decision to respect those boundaries must have broken his heart; he must have thought, in some small way, that I had hated Leena enough to help him. Jackie shifted the thin paper bag in her arms. Of Leena and Julian, she said she knew little, except that Leena had visited her briefly sometime in February, and there was still no news of Julian.

On the way home, I drove past their house. It was unlit, and the unfinished sections had dilapidated further, perhaps due to plain neglect. Its shadowed face greeted the rest of the neighborhood like a lonely moan. Dead brush engulfed Julian's now barren garden, which sat invisible in the dark. The windows were like black water. Leena's remaining ornaments clung to the thin, metal edge above the entrance, clinking in the push and pull of wind. Leaves congregated in the corner of the bare porch, while others scattered, scratching the concrete driveway. The cactuses near the wall that divided part of the front yard lay in a perfect arc, a slow dive into the grass where they resumed their careful process of rotting. There weren't any FOR SALE signs, no marks of visitation. It was like a cold star. Would they come back to claim it? Would it return to its former, unshakeable assertion about the world? I drove away from the house, and a strange clarity came the further away I got from it. It was absorbed by the other well-lit homes along the street. It was loud in its anonymity, something anyone could see.

BOWL-HEAD

The woman wasn't visible from the street corner.

Justin only saw the traffic stopped at the light when he stepped from the curb with three other pedestrians; it was a short distance to the next curb, and he caught a glimpse of the sun bursting around the edges of a building, too bright in the winter clouds, which were long gray streaks. They grew darker near the horizon where wet concrete met the vanishing point of the street, promising another night of freezing slush. Exhaust billowed from the backs of taxis lined at the crosswalk.

With a modicum of disgust, Justin passed a pile of damp clothing on wilted cardboard boxes. A red sweatshirt lay on top, arms splayed, and it struck him as odd; it was the only thing of color that stood out on the street. Beads of moisture glistened on the front of it. Inexplicably pulled toward the shirt, Justin entertained his irrational attraction to it, and he gently rested his hand in the center of the beads pooled there. The beads combined into tiny ovals, then soaked all the way into the fabric, making a dark stain where it went in. Lifting his hand somehow brought him back to the street, to his need to get home; Cal was waiting, and he was already late.

She had expressed doubts about them lately. Her ad hoc explanation to him at 4:00 AM focused almost exclusively on "healthy selfishness," "blood moons," and "generating relationship abundance," whatever-the-fuck that was, and it left his mouth dry and his legs weak. Her expectations manifested like invisible weights, each connected to a different part of him. When he thought of his own expectations, he drew a blank; it was as though her suppositions had become his. He wondered if he would tell her about the red sweatshirt, and then his stomach turned on itself, and he knew he shouldn't be that intimate with her. She wouldn't understand, especially when he didn't understand it, the jolting, almost magnetic pull toward it. This shirt somehow seemed like the opposite of Cal for a minute, and perhaps that's what explained things; its receptivity, its openness, even though it was just a shirt. But he did care for her; his ego didn't benefit from any nudges upwards considering that she depended on him to help her in and out of the bath, sometimes to dress, sometimes to undress.

They both went to see the demolished cab in the junkyard together when she came back, cast-bound, bandaged, and wrapped in white straps, her face shaded deep red in the corners of her eyes near the bridge of her nose, which was stitched jaggedly up the center. Her cheeks were creased with scars like a knife tried to cut Cs into them, or little moons. The place where they had pried and pulled her from the metal curled backward like leaves. When she examined it, leaving Justin a few feet behind to watch, she looked like she was searching for someone inside, as if someone was still down in there needing to be pulled out, rescued.

"Let's go." Justin said, hoping it would be easy for her to say yes.

"One more minute." Cal didn't look at him when she

said this. Instead she stared through the cracks splintering the windshield.

"It's too cold," she told him, then said she wanted to leave.

Back at their apartment, he asked her if she wanted to go to the cab driver's funeral. Cal never responded, even as he stood there waiting. She sat at the dining table peeling an orange, and Justin noticed that she did it slowly, each piece a potential trigger, the fruit inside like a delicate bomb. Bathing her was a chore, and not the loving, sensual experience he predicted it would become. Later on, he chided himself for being an absurd romantic, naive even. Cal was fussy, like a child dictating where he should put the soap, how much he should put on the sponge. When he used it, her body turned unpredictable, at once eliciting moans of thick pleasure, but one move to the next territory of skin and outrage took over. She blamed him for it; the pitfalls of her body were his fault. Each pain was an explosion across the now vague map of her limbs, and each produced tears that only underlined the scarring, and it made him afraid to lift the sponge, or to step across the room to retrieve a towel. Helping her from the tub and into her robe was a revelation of how healing actually works. It was awkward, indifferent. Parts sealed back together like a blind kid correcting a brief mistake. It was humiliating, he thought, the way a body tried to hide anything broken, the way each knob of her spine showed up like white pebbles in the black-red streak stretching from her neck to her tailbone. It was so dark, Justin thought it looked like paint, or as if Cal had soaked in tar and cherry juice for months. When it bled, and it did, it resembled pulped fruit, especially when Cal bent at the slightest.

In bed, every light had to be turned on, and three distinct pillows had to be used to prop her up. Her right leg had to be at a specific angle, while the left had to be forward. She said this helped her spine, although Justin wasn't sure how it worked. The books she read before sleep had to be changed regularly, and when the pain was really bad, she demanded he read chapters to her, thus neglecting his own reading. If he fell asleep first, usually due to fatigue, he heard about it in the morning: *How dare you leave me awake alone for so long when you know the pills usher in some pretty uncompromising insomnia, Justin.* What was *she* supposed to do, she would ask him, when a book fell from her lap to the floor and all she had to look at were her hands, or the wall?

Sometimes the trauma of the crash visited her in her dreams and Justin didn't sleep at all when she woke him, screaming in a long guttural howl. The winter made it worse for both of them; he believed his body ached in tandem with hers, a crude kind of symbiosis, phantom throbs in his lower back where he imagined he'd hit it on something, or the dull pangs up to his wrists that stopped right at his elbows. When the sky darkened at five in the afternoon, the aches didn't waste any time.

But now, standing by the red sweatshirt and the pile of clothes, the street took priority over his thoughts. Part of the gray buildings receded inward, away from the curb, which revealed a set of stairs inside an open foyer. Black and white tile covered the floor. He noticed a closed register desk. The place must have been a hotel at one point, he figured, noting water leaking in puddles across the tile.

That's when the woman showed up, the one he didn't notice before, watching him down the block. She was gray and hunched. Her back had the shape of a cashew. Her clothing was the same gray as the building, except with a greenish tint, and something lavender just under the surface. Her face resembled a balled-up knee; it bunched together with pale, white cheeks filling up around the odd triangle of her chin, and her eyes covered over, hidden because her brow was too prominent.

Her ashy blond hair looked thin. It was capped in a tight brown cloth, and the mittens on her hands lacked fingers at the tips. She waved at Justin, ushering him into the foyer. The woman spoke, and Justin had to lean close to listen: "Come on, come on, let's go, we gotta go, now. Okay? We gotta go, come on." She preceded him up the stairs. He followed her to see what she wanted. "Come on," she said. "We have to hurry. Come now."

•

Attempting to heed the warning in his chest, Justin stopped on the landing while the woman continued to march up the steps. He stared at her hunched back, the round meaty shake of her sides.

"Ma'am," he said, his tone imploring her to stop. "Ma'am. Is there someone you need, someone I should get for you?"

The woman didn't answer him, but he noticed a slight pause in her rush to get upstairs. He thought he saw disappointment in the way she stood. *What am I doing by following this woman?* She turned to look down at him. "If you don't come, then no one will," she said, and the look in her scrunched up face broke through his reserve. He followed her up the rest of the steps to a small, curved hall with four doors. She went to the second one from the left. He maintained a distance that he hoped wouldn't be seen as rude. Her hands jangled the keys. A skylight caked in debris and leaves filtered weak, rainy light over the hall. A few pigeons fluttered across the webbed glass. When she had the door open, she waved Justin inside, her gloved hand like a claw. He followed her and she shut the door behind him.

Across from the door were four windows, each producing the same watery light from the hall. Under the windows against the wall was a small couch with gray-green, felt cushions, and no pillows. A tiny wooden table stood near the entrance and the woman dropped her keys into a glass dish in the shape of a duck. Its face smiled up at Justin with incongruous hilarity, something he found oddly telling about this woman, and the home he'd just entered. The rest of the decorations were as sparse as the couch. A couple of tiny pictures hung on the wall on either side of the sliding wooden doors to his left. They were parted but not enough to see what was inside. He remained in the foyer like a respectful guest, and also a fearful one. He felt safer near the door, although the woman seemed innocuous. What could she do to him? He wondered what Cal must be thinking right now; he also wondered if he was doing this on purpose to draw things out, to make her wait. Standing silently in the entrance of this woman's apartment he hoped that he was wrong.

The woman approached Justin with an awkward slowness. Her face was still hooded, bunched together, her brow so large it was like her eyes were trying to hide deep inside her skull, even if he caught glimpses of them. The first thing he thought upon further observation with her this close to him was that she resembled a toad; it wasn't nice, but that's what she resembled, and her hunched, balled body didn't help. The turban on her head was so snug he wondered if she ever took it off. It looked like it was part of her, sealed to the round bulbous curve of her skull. Justin looked down and saw her hands were bare, the gloves gone somewhere, and she held them, fingertip-to-fingertip, evoking a gentle, embarrassed modestly.

Hesitant to ask, for fear of what he'd gotten himself into, Justin waited before inquiring what it was the woman wanted. He figured she would tell him, or at least offer some kind of nicety like stale cookies, payment to help her fix something: leaky faucets, a cabinet that wouldn't close. But this wasn't it at all. He might have preferred those things to what came next and to what he had, by default of entering her apartment, obligated himself. She was shy to ask him, and he was try-ing to think of various explanations for why he should leave. His hands were slick and his stomach twisted, standing there, looking at her; did he really pity her, this poor, hunched woman, her mouth opening and closing with a wet click while she tried to get it out?

"I need you," she said. Her voice was a stretched croak. Also frog-like, he thought, then winced, and stepped back a bit. "I need you to try my bowl."

"I'm sorry?" Justin blurted.

"I need you to try my bowl."

She waited for him to respond further, and he wasn't sure what to say.

"Your bowl?"

"My bowl."

"I'm not sure I understand. But if you could elabo-rate…"

"Here," she told him. "Sit. This way. Sit."

The more she spoke, the more her throat-rattle be-trayed an accent, something Polish, was it? He found himself wanting her to speak more so he could detect it accurately, or at least decide if he was imagining an accent. He followed her and took a seat on the small couch under the windows, which would have fit well inside a French parlor, or a much nicer sitting room than this. The carvings in the wood were smooth, he noticed, and showed faded gold. Justin started to ask her where she got it, and where she had come from, when she left the room. He clasped his workbag. His brown hair hung in his face. He felt ridiculous sitting there, waiting, reduced almost, and not sure where the feeling came from.

When the woman returned, she brought with her a giant glass bowl that filled both of her arms. He imagined her trying to carry a watermelon, and it had the same effect. It looked like it was made of sea glass and contained multiple bubbles and cracks inside it. There was a metal rim around its edge. Justin's instinct was to help the woman with it, but something in her movements said she could carry it just fine. She put it right in the center of the small wooden table before the couch. It wobbled a bit when she lifted her arms from it, then stretched slightly, emitting a grunt.

"That's my bowl," she said, and he thought he could discern a smile somewhere in her bunched face.

"Your bowl," said Justin. "Is there something wrong with it? You seemed like you were in an emergency earlier."

"It is. It's an emergency," she said. Her hands clasped again, school-girlish. She looked down at the wooden floors.

"Okay," Justin began. "Tell me how I can help you."

"Put it on."

"Put it on? Like, on my head?"

"Put it on, yes. And you will help me."

"I don't think that will work. I'm sorry. That thing—well, it's so big, it could hurt my neck."

"Not hurt your neck. Magda promise. I'm Magda."

"Nice to meet you, Magda."

He tried to think of a way to get out of this, the full tumult of regret hitting him now.

"Stay," said Magda. "Sit. Put on the bowl. I will help. If the bowl fall, I will catch it. Okay? Now put on the bowl. For Magda, please."

The sense of obligation rolled around in him again, and he wanted to crush it; a bowl? Really?

"Okay," he said. "Okay, I'll put it on. But I'll need your help to lift it."

The woman leaned forward, grunting, and with both arms she lifted the bowl up and over to him, where he took it like a baby. Then he lifted it, feeling its weight, which was not as heavy as he predicted. Justin turned the bowl upside down and placed it on top of his head, keeping his hands on either side just to manage its weight.

"Okay, now what?"

He stared through the glass bubbles, and the room distorted; parts of it seemed to swirl across the glass, the walls mutating into paste, and then a light came on, orange and yellow at the center; it was across the room from him. Its color sluiced over the glass, mixing with the mutations of the furniture and windows, the wooden sliding doors. His hearing was somewhat distorted in the bowl, but he could still pick out Magda. She was walking away from him, across the room, now, and she stood near the doors. Her shape had, unsurprisingly, become mutated as well, although it was an even more hunched version of herself. Magda had shrunk, while the doors seemed to enlarge and blur in the orange light. Justin's hands were slick. He was getting tired of holding the bowl. He found himself tilting it, even squinting through striations and chips among the clustered orbs within the glass to see what she was doing. He froze and listened. She was whispering, telling someone on the other side of the doors something. Someone else was here? A tiny shape came—or *bloomed* was a better word—into the space between the doors, right next to Magda.

Justin could make out blond hair and pale skin. Whoever it was, they stared at him. This went on for a while, and Justin began to call Magda's name. He heard her, finally. That same throaty, creaking voice: "See," she said, like a mother to a child when it first glimpses something miraculous, but simple: a sunset, a meteor falling. "See…"

The person vanished behind the doors when Justin stopped calling for Magda. He could hear the doors shut, and the determined clop of Magda's feet echoed across the wooden floor to where he sat.

"Okay," she said. "Okay, you take it off now."

Justin lifted the bowl from his head, and cool air met his face. Feelings of strained emptiness filled him where he'd expected relief to be, then low-grade shock followed; he suddenly didn't want to let go of the bowl, or stop being inside it. She looked at him from underneath her brow. Her toad lips pursed in a vague expression of approval. The feeling it gave Justin was that he had met her needs, and then some. But how? What had he done, exactly? What had happened here?

"You helped. You can go now."

"That's it? That's what you needed?" Justin felt very small, even as he tried to sound useful. It was as though he had been lectured the same way an adult lectures a child who enjoyed a brief, idiosyncratic trespass, and was asked to go to his room. He thought to inquire if he had done something wrong, but hesitated instead.

Gathering his things, he stood and shuffled toward the front door, half turning a couple of times to look at the bowl on the table, longing for the weight of it again. It rested in the warmth of the orange lamp in the corner. He quickly glanced at the two sliding doors, then right back to the bowl.

At the door, he was surprised to hear himself tell Magda that if she needed him to come again, he would, and he would wear the bowl again, if it helped, any time.

"You can go now," was all she said, and her voice was less croaky. It was smoother, resigned.

Magda grasped the handle and opened the door for Justin, who walked into the curved hallway. He refused to look at the set of stairs leading back down to the street. Magda gave a brief nod through the crack in the door before she shut it, which shook the wall and startled the pigeons in the corners of the skylight above him.

•

For weeks following the incident at Magda's apartment, Justin began engaging in the surreptitious practice of placing bowls on his head and assuming a slight meditative stance, whether sitting or standing. The bowls varied in size, and some were dog bowls from years past; they were plastic, red and yellow, and fit the top of his head like an awkward yammaka. He managed to keep the practice secret, usually standing in the kitchen with the new mixing bowl Cal ordered from Williams-Sonoma balanced on the crown of his head. He began ordering them himself, and the collection grew, much to Cal's stupefaction. She still hadn't forgiven him for being late that night, returning with a ridiculous story about traffic and strange weather; but in light of this new, idiosyncratic development, she had forgiven him, and not because she found it endearing, but because it scared her, and if she was less sure of things before, she was even more certain of their shakiness now.

Justin's fascination with bowls didn't stop at simple online ordering, but continued into the public sphere, where he subjected Cal to long shopping tirades seeking out "bowls with imperfections," going through stacks of them in various textile stores, while she observed his feverish searching. Justin was grateful she never approached him about the bowl hunts, or his burgeoning fascination with them. He noticed that it alienated her, and while he was concerned that it might wound their relationship later, he was glad for it now; and there was another side to this, which he rarely admitted to himself, which was the revenge of it. Yes, he felt avenged. There was a distinct thrill to her marginalization. He knew it wasn't right, exactly, but after all she'd put him through during her thankless recovery, Justin savored this crude type of severance; he had managed to remove himself from Cal, yet also remained right by her side. He knew her well enough, too; she'd never really ask him about what was happening with the bowls. She hadn't witnessed him putting them on his head. She wasn't there for his sudden slowed heart rate, the quiet drop of his spinal muscles as he relinquished himself to the incomparable feeling of a bowl on top of his head; she'd seen nothing until he got sloppy. He confused dates once, and didn't realize she'd only gone out to get coffee. She returned to their apartment so softly the door didn't make a sound upon her entrance. When he saw her staring at him in the kitchen, he startled, and the glass bowl on his head fell straight to the ground, bursting into thick shards everywhere as Cal's firm voice let loose in the room: "What the hell are you doing?"

He looked down at the broken mess around his bare feet, then up at her.

Justin thought her black hair seemed tighter than usual, pulled back the way it was, and that her face was narrower.

She left him standing there in the kitchen and said nothing more that day.

•

There wasn't any discussion about what Cal had caught Justin doing in the kitchen, which he'd anticipated. It was as if she'd resigned herself to the mystery of it. Cal maintained a silence that was worse than the enigma of his bowl obsession. Maybe she wanted revenge, too. Whatever it was, she refused to include him in it. But he watched her. Like tonight, she ran a bath for herself, quietly moving about the bathroom, pouring potions and salts into the roaring water. She even hummed to herself. As he watched, he noticed she did not appear to see him at all. He thought he might make himself useful, might offer to help her into the bath, or to dry her. But he knew this would not work, and it would appear desperate, even pitiful; she would see through it. And since she'd healed, she'd become adept at managing a bath on her own. Cal could do things by herself again. But she did ask him to bring her a towel.

Looking at her body in the dim bathroom light, he could still see lines all over it. The dark spot at the top of her left shoulder when he'd first got her home was prominent; how long did they spend there, massaging it, moving her arm to keep the muscle tone up? There was the plump scar at the base of her spine; they'd spent about a week on that one, applying ointments and other medications squeezed from a tube to make sure infection didn't get in. It had been one of the bigger openings. He remembered the caution he took dabbing liquids onto the raw split in her flesh, all woven together with black stitches, something she couldn't see because she had to look the other way. Every movement was an act of trust; Cal had temporarily given her body to him to fix. But what choice did she get? Justin thought of all relationships like this, a companionable victimhood where you allowed yourself to become an object for a while, the only betrayal of which could be ingratitude; a pact was made with your bodies, with the rooms you occupied, and the idea of the thing you created remained hidden.

•

Sometimes Justin found himself near Magda's apartment during the week. He would tell himself that he returned there by accident. He ate in restaurants down the street and watched the gray entrance to the building, the people moving quickly past it, unaware and unfazed by its presence. How could they not see it, or *sense* it, he often thought to himself, disbelievingly, and then realized, why would they? They hadn't been there; they hadn't seen what he'd seen. He wanted to recreate the incident in the apartment, the donning of the bowl, and the feeling that came from it, including the visions he saw, which came after.

When he had initially left Magda's apartment that day, the street appeared to him normally. It was a few blocks later that it began to change. First came a dance of particles, which he could see like bright motes, then the dissolution of them and himself. His body became absorbed into a type of green nebulae shattering in on itself right there in the middle of the street, simultaneously imploding and moving outwards, and no one saw it but him. That was as far as he got in his memory of it, every time. But the feeling was still there, and there was more, wasn't there?

Surely, there was more.

•

Justin eventually returned to the apartment carrying a plastic sack. He stood in front of the door, and the pigeons that normally rustled over the skylight were nowhere to be seen. Dried leaves had taken their place, scratching against the glass. The stairwell had a new coat of paint on it. Justin knocked politely, then braced himself. He wondered how he would take the bowl, if he would just rush in and steal it, or threaten Magda until she gave it to him. But there was no response, and he felt an instinctive panic that she was not home. He tried again. Still nothing. Justin leaned against the door and toyed with the doorknob petulantly until it turned too much for a locked door. Justin kept turning it until the latch came back and the door opened into the apartment. He stood there and waited for someone to come forward when he noticed that the room was entirely bare, the elaborate couch gone. A few slivers of old newspaper remained on the wooden floors.

He stepped inside and called out a cursory hello. But there was no response. The kitchen was empty, and the room behind the sliding doors was also stripped of any furniture or belongings. The place had been abandoned, as if they had only been here temporarily, perhaps on a month-to-month basis, even. Justin didn't know. His first thought was that he could try to find them, to track them down. But he wasn't sure that would result in anything except suspicion, and all he wanted was the bowl anyway. He sat on the bare floor right where the couch had been and he first put the bowl on his head. If he tried to recreate the experience before, he really tried now, but it was fruitless. The emptiness of the room, the sound of the wind moving through it from an open window, these things won out, and he couldn't concentrate. Wind screeched past the building, a draft of which entered and sent newspaper pages drifting toward him; the ghostly quality of it didn't escape Justin. Neither did the feeling that something happened here, something he'd missed, and the residue of it hung around. He didn't want to know what it was, if it was anything.

In the kitchen, he looked around. The sink was full of nails and dirt. In the pantry on the floor, under the nearest shelf, was a brown paper bag. He leaned inside to open it up. There, in the bottom, he saw the bowl, shattered into a hundred pieces.

•

Cal packed all her belongings and left Justin two days after she caught him attempting to glue the bowl back together at the kitchen table. Some parts of it had been pulverized to dust, which left huge gaps for Justin to fill. He sat shirtless, his skin ashen and sweaty. His brown hair had taken on the same flat quality, as if it had been dusted with the pulverized glass in the plastic bag. His fingers were raw and bled, and they itched in the creases. Small cuts formed along his knuckles. He sucked and licked the cuts, getting bits of grit in his mouth, swallowing anyway, then continuing his work. He didn't mind if pieces of it got inside him; he wanted them there. He had half of the bowl reconstructed. It lay like an egg shell, a crooked C-shape. Some of the bubbles in the glass were incorrect, and he knew he had glued wrong pieces together, but he didn't care. He pressed on anyway until he had it almost completed; the gist of the bowl was there, right in front of him. When he looked into the bag, he only saw more dust, and feared the larger parts of it—the ones he needed to create full cohesion—were all just dust now.

He let what he had completed dry for three days. He ate at the table where he could look at it, and left a circle of dirty bowls on the floor around his chair; the same ones he and Cal had bought together, the plastic red dog bowls, and the ones from furniture stores, including the ones that were meant to emulate the fractal one on the table. He left them there. They fanned out and filled the room, pocked and caked in everything he'd consumed. When he ran out of them, he ate with his hands. And when there wasn't any food left, he didn't eat. His skin draped on his bones, and the ghosts of blue veins showed through the surface. His skull became prominent, a waxy crag. Soon he would have a rictus. The weight of the bowl pressed deep into his palms when he lifted it, admiring the sutures running through its cracked surface. In the emptiness of the apartment, he heard people outside. Someone was talking. He wondered if it was Cal; did she forget something, a remaining bottle of her scar lotion, perhaps? He didn't know. Had she ever really been in the apartment? He thought he could hear her, right there, in the other room. The bowl was here, however, and it was his, whatever shape it took.

THE EXCHANGE

Some people swore that the house was haunted. But, perhaps that's because the house asked more of them than they were willing to give. Its location in the center of the block was unavoidable. Every day people walked past it, their heads lowered, dogs in tow. Sometimes, when I visited, I watched them.

Neighbors never complained to the city that its dead grass be mowed, or that a paint job was past due. It was avoided. It existed only when others wanted it; a reminder of what they were not. Of course, the house remained empty most of the year, its original owners all dead now. It was unclear to me why it hadn't been sold or torn down. As far as I knew I had the last key. I visited to remind myself I had been a part of it. The family that once occupied the house were my neighbors. Their children, Tyler and Matilde, were my only friends, and most of my childhood consisted of us inside their house making rooms out of rooms. My own home became secondary to theirs. It appeared to promise things with its long, dimly lit halls, ceilings that seemed to rise and rise, and fireplaces like charred, hungry mouths.

My visits to the house began with Tyler. He brought me there to show me how limitless it was, how the rest of the world stopped when you crossed its threshold. Three stories of space in which to hide, rooms that went unchecked. I became as intimate with it as Tyler allowed me. I soon learned that parts of it had been divided into territories. It was unspoken but Matilde kept her distance, and I rarely saw them share the same domain for longer than a few minutes.

I never questioned this as long as I was allowed to be near Tyler; he lived disconnected, reckless. Proximity to him pulled at something in my gut. It seemed that he knew this, but pretended otherwise. The night he called for me I went over immediately. The front door was left unlocked. I entered and took the stairs two at a time until I reached his floor. I knocked on his bedroom door and waited. He opened it a fraction, his room barely lit behind him. His smile exposed caution as if he were checking to make sure nothing had changed. Tyler leaned forward and kissed me. He pulled back fast leaving the inside of my bottom lip raw. I didn't move but wanted him to do it again. I believe he anticipated this, and he let the door fall open so I could see inside the room. On his bed lay Matilde, face down, dark red pouring along folds in the sheets from under her neck. In the orange light of his desk lamp sat an open straight razor.

"Help me," said Tyler.

He ran a finger across the back of my neck then gestured at Matilde, unmoving. It was an extension of the kiss. I understood what he wanted me to do, what was expected. It occurred to me that the kiss at the door was now a kind of currency.

Nothing was ever the same again after that.

GOD'S GLORIOUS SPLENDOR!

Someone shot the peacock. Everything followed after that.

Nancy was the first to notice it at 6:00 AM when it was still alive and waltzing in its particular strut, up and down the slopes of her roof, unsure of how it got out and how it got up there. She leaned down to pick up the paper—her home was one of the few on the long stretch of road that still got one—and when she turned, there it was, its giant tail partially fanned in the orange light of that early, September morning. Nancy hated mornings, and believed getting up before 11:00 AM led to an early death. Kevin, her husband, insisted that she had it all wrong, and she resented him for this; early risers got more out of life, he told her—they had higher sex drives, made more money, and they smiled. She humored him by doing this early morning act of getting the newspaper. She didn't understand what anyone got from being exhausted, and she derived secret pleasure seeing Kevin this way, sagging with fatigue when he opened the door at 8:00 each night, arriving home after a two-hour stay at the gym: innumerable rounds of cardio, intermittent fasting, ice packs for the swelling, and an hour of work on his phone spent emailing his clueless clients. He never stopped. Nancy saw his vision of sleep as an inconvenience, whereas to her, sleep was a kind of sanctuary. Kevin also wanted to build things by hand, like the shed in their backyard. It resembled a vague accident, or a ruin, thought Nancy. A stretch of their yard smeared in cement dust, a half-assed job of pouring a mixture into a grid Kevin spent seven hours demarcating, only for it to resemble a shape she couldn't decipher—it was just there. He managed to get the start of the brick work accomplished, then stopped abruptly to begin something new, casting off the shed as though it wasn't his, but someone else's mistake. Nancy occasionally noticed him staring at it with an odd sort of confusion in his eyes, like he didn't understand what it was any more than she did. She couldn't decide if he was annoyed with it, or if he had other plans he would eventually implement later. He had spoken of building a garage apartment by hand, and then later decided it should be a tiny house with a secret shelter underneath. She was intrigued by the concept, but when she asked him what it would contain, he accused her of being condescending, and left quickly for the gym.

Nancy got a call from her neighbor, Jill, who lived on an acreage a mile or two away from theirs; she was the first to tell Nancy about the peacock, which was part of a small llama farm on the acreage of their other neighbors, the Watsons, who seldom spoke to anybody.

"You can't believe it! You've got to see it for yourself! You've got to!"

Jill shouted at Nancy with an emotion she hadn't heard in a while, a form of stunned awe. The fact that this bird existed, and that she'd witnessed it, seemed to have brought Jill to another level of consciousness beyond her online aromatherapy sales, and her glitter-stitch purses with crucifixes sparkling in the center of faux, pink leather. Sometimes there was a crown of thorns, and she admitted to the thought of making another version with hands, a hole in each one to signify the stigmata, and a 'T' through the holes, to signify Trump.

"Jesus and Trump are my best guys!" She often said this as a pathway to assess the guests who sometimes showed up to her neighborhood cookouts. How she decided four houses with bordering acreages constituted a neighborhood was a question Nancy left unexplored.

She eventually went on her own to see the peacock, and later learned it had a name: Mr. Peacock. Mr. Watson's earnestness caused Nancy's knees to go weak with embarrassment, but she convinced him the name was "creative" and "adorable." The bird, on the other hand, seemed to search for something, looking out beyond the fence line, as if it had been torn away from a lover or had eggs hatching somewhere, left vulnerable to vipers or other predators. It didn't care that they were there, staring at it. It pranced, thought Nancy, like a prissy king, or more accurately, like it'd been sequestered at the Holiday Inn of pens, and couldn't believe the service, the food, or the other idiots sharing it.

Jill had a different idea of the peacock. She took all four neighbors out to dinner, and then drove them back to the Watson's farm, where she produced a sign and stuck it into the ground directly in front of the fence line. It read: GOD'S GLORIOUS SPLENDOR! For Jill's sake, Nancy smiled, clapping her hands to her chest to show some kind of excitement, even if it was manufactured. She looked at the others standing there, her husband, all of them graciously giving Jill her moment. Nancy wondered how patient they would have been had Jill not just treated them to a 300 dollar steak dinner. Nancy looked to Mr. Watson, whose face took on a grayish color and a restrained expression of concern as Jill seemed to forget who owned the bird, and cooed at it, as it wandered farther away from them, distracted by something at the far corner of the pen. Jill's voice became more baby-like, more high-pitched, but everyone just stood there, waiting, as if she had another surprise to spring on them, another sign for the Watson's yard. Nancy tried not to stare at Mr. Watson, but it was difficult; she considered how long he would keep the sign Jill had stuck there with its kindergarten clouds, letters in alternating colors of purple, green, and blue, and a tiny pink crucifix at a diagonal in the bottom, right-hand corner.

The problem was that it could be seen from the road, even at a distance of a few miles, thus obligating Mr. Watson to keep it there, or risk upsetting Jill's good intentions by removing it. When Jill turned to look at them, her face was flushed and her eyes searched them like someone about to turn fanatic. She went to her husband, Mark, and aggressively pawed at his jacket pockets.

"Where's the feed, Mark? Where is it?"

"I don't know, Jill."

Tears formed on her pink face, and she pushed past him.

"I'll be in the car," she mumbled.

"Is she okay?" Nancy asked.

"She's fine. She's just tired. Goodnight, you all," said Mark.

Jill and Mark sped away in their Range Rover that looked more like a tactical vehicle than an actual car.

The rest of them dispersed. Mr. Watson went inside. Kevin and Nancy climbed into their maroon Audi. Kevin sped away too fast for Nancy to see at what distance the sign could be viewed. Kevin surprised her by dropping her off at the house, and then going to the gym for a few hours. She had hoped they might do something together, discuss Jill, maybe. Kevin's disinterest surpassed his usual flatline reactions. She wondered why she was the only one to see that something was wrong with Jill, something that had been there a while. After a bath and a glass of stale wine, Nancy forgot about Jill, too, and instead focused on her cooking and make-up vlog. She'd been creating content for three years, now. She had only 50 followers, but thought more might come. She practiced visualization techniques, and frequently read *The Secret* to remind herself of the Law of Attraction. She wrote and meditated about her energy field, unsure if it was repellent or clogged in some way. She scribbled in the white light of her kitchen, on the white granite counter, the metal bar stool, cold under her bare ass, while her white robe slid open at the chest. She saw her energy field as purple, like the peacock, like its feathers. It had an energy field, too, she decided, and thought perhaps she shared a connection with it. While writing this down, she heard a Ping! as an email came through. It was Jill requesting Nancy to like her newly created Facebook page, the words: God's Glorious Splendor! in taupe across the top of the page. A shaky phone pic of the peacock taken from behind the Watson's fence was the only picture. So far, there were two likes, including Nancy's. She exhaled and was caught off guard by how bereft she sounded.

"Oh Jill," she muttered.

She exhaled again, as if trying to get rid of the gravity taking up space in her sternum. She shut her computer, and went to bed, still wrapped in her white robe. The wine glass on the bedside table was drained. The marble lamp cast a sheen over her lip marks on the rim. She noticed there were overlays where her mouth had pressed repeatedly, refusing to drink from any other side of the glass. Her mouth made it look ugly, she thought. Before she fell asleep, she caught the sound of the clock in the kitchen. The house was quiet, and Kevin still hadn't come back from the gym. 50 followers. She groaned and curled into herself. Fifty… A sense of worthlessness crept in right before sleep hit.

When she woke, it was 9:00 AM, and the sound of Kevin taking a loud crap was the first thing she heard. Her phone was green with text messages from her sister, Sky, in Manitou Springs. Sky's son, Ben, needed to stay with her for a few days on his way to New York for school. She had posed this like a question but, in the last message, said he was already on his way.

"Kevin?"

"Yeah?"

"Ben is coming to stay with us."

"The nephew?"

"Yeah."

"Why?"

"He's on his way to New York. For school."

"Sky tell you that?"

"Yeah."

"Can you say no?"

"No."

"Why not?"

"Cause. He's family."

"This is the gay one, right?"

"Yes, Kevin."

"Does he know we don't have any gays here?"

Nancy ignored this, and got up.

"Nancy. Does he know?"

In the kitchen, she checked her email, her vlog, and Facebook. Jill's fan page for the Watson's bird now had 110 likes. Nancy shut her laptop, a cold rage taking over. 110 likes for that? She wearily noted her vlog had no views today.

Ben arrived on Tuesday afternoon and parked his white Honda down the drive, rather than near the front door. Why he did this, Nancy couldn't figure, but Kevin, who had managed to be home, answered the door and showed Ben inside. Nancy greeted him in the kitchen, where he set his overnight bag in a chair by the bar. He was plain, thought Nancy. Very plain. He wore regular jeans, a long-sleeved workout shirt, and tennis shoes. His hair, which was shaved up one side, was the only thing about him that was unique. She felt disappointed, and wasn't sure why, and then feared that introducing him to the others, like Jill, wouldn't be as fun as if he were, what—more eccentric? She imagined Jill's reaction upon inevitably learning from Kevin that Ben is an out member of the LGTBQ+ community. Her last remark, Nancy never forgot: "How many letters do they *actually* need?"

"We'll let you get settled," said Kevin. "If you need anything, go for it. Hey, by the way, I don't know if you know this, but Nancy watches 'Queer Eyes,' and she has a make-up blog, or vlog, or whatever it's called."

Ben nodded. "Great," he said.

"Thanks for that, Kevin," said Nancy, her voice conveying both a sense of humiliation on Kevin's behalf, and an unspoken, *Are you fucking kidding me?*

Ben went upstairs to his room after a polite 'thank you' to both of them, seemingly unaware of the exchange between Nancy and Kevin.

"Jesus, Kevin."

"What?"

"Are you serious or just trying to be an asshole?"

"What are you talking about? I thought he'd like to know you're cool."

"That I'm *cool*?"

Kevin stood in silence at this, like a dog realizing that it was wrong, after all, to have shit in mommy's shoe.

"I don't know, Kevin, do you go up to your black co-workers and tell them you're up on BET?"

He stayed mute, oddly, and seemed unable to decide where to go.

"We're trash," said Nancy, partly to herself, fury manifesting in her face like an eruption of late stage rosacea. "We're fucking trash."

Saying nothing, Kevin walked into the bedroom and grabbed his black gym bag, then walked back down the hall and out of the front door, slamming it with a firm, but strangely measured clap that echoed up to the ceiling. Nancy then got a text from Jill asking her to help fundraise for God's Glorious Splendor, so he could have a pen of his own. Fundraise? Nancy bit the insides of her cheeks. The notion was absurd. Jill's husband could buy the bird multiple pens with what he made. Nancy's ribs burned, her hands clenched. It made her think Jill just wanted an excuse to have a fundraiser; it didn't matter what it was for. If she really wanted the peacock to have its own pen, she could go buy one right now. Nancy texted a short, polite reply that she was busy. She mentioned Ben, and Jill insisted Nancy bring him to their cookout on Wednesday. Nancy said she'd run it by him, but thought it might be better if she kept him here the whole time. The urge to protect Ben suddenly overwhelmed her. To move past this bizarre, new emotion, she logged into her website to check views. Still nothing. Jill's fan page, however, was up to 370 likes. Where the hell are they coming from? Nancy asked herself this and took half a Xanax.

An hour later, Ben came down the stairs looking more rested, and seemingly unperturbed by what Kevin had said to him. He told Nancy he was starving, and asked if any restaurants were nearby that he could drive to.

"Don't be silly," she said. "I'll make you something. It'll just be you and me, I'm afraid."

Ben offered to help, and Nancy refused, instead turning on the TV for him. A nature channel played. Ben watched it quietly. He was so quiet, Nancy almost forgot he was sitting a few feet from her, until he changed the channel, and she heard him mutter approval over an action movie. She finished the salmon, which she brought to him where he sat. Together, they ate and watched the movie. When it was over, Ben took his plate to the sink, then went to his room, thanking her again.

"Any time, Ben," she said, and took her usual seat at the kitchen bar.

Nancy didn't check the computer. Instead, she just sat there. She tried to drink her wine, but that proved difficult. The ticking clock was loud again. She felt as though the walls of the house were gone; that the expanse of the black fields going for miles around them were, in fact, *her*; she'd become that space, she decided—an endless circumference, a suggestion of something, but nothing more than that. The cold of that dark place was her, too. Somehow, this had to do with Ben visiting, with his innocuous, polite, 'good night' to her; and the fact that he'd be gone in less than 48 hours. Kevin came home a few minutes later, and approached her in the kitchen, incredulous.

"You made fish?"

His eyes widened, his shoulders slumped. She could see a 10 year old version of him, dejected, entitled. She held a separate vision of his mother, suddenly.

"There's a little left if you want it," she told him, and went to bed.

The cookout at Jill's included tiki-torches. Nancy thought it was predictable, but it worked somehow, sputtering thick flames around a buffet. There was even a centerpiece: a cake with a giant peacock drawn right in the center. No wording, just the peacock, which surprised Nancy because she figured Jill would want to show off the name she gave the bird at every opportunity. Her husband's work friends, their wives and kids, and some high school friends of Jill's made up most of the crowd. Nancy admired Jill's unevolved relationships—how, despite Jill's friends going to college, and ostensibly moving on, Jill kept them tethered. Since she married right out of high school, college was thrown out before it could even be considered. Jill told Nancy about the miscarriages, four in one year before they'd met. After that, they'd stopped trying. Later, it occurred to Nancy the one thing all four neighbors had in common was that they were childless. How was this not obvious before? She turned to look at the decimated peacock cake on the table.

Ben stayed near the buffet, eating celery sticks and staring into his phone. Nancy had already paraded him around, introduced him to people he didn't care to meet and would never see again. She noted his plainness once more, his banality. She was shocked to hear him say he was going to study playwriting to one of Jill's lawyers, who stared at him, chewing a mouthful of the cake, which turned his lips purple from the icing. Ben appeared mildly stoic, the way she would imagine a data scientist or computer science major, but not a playwright.

"Are you writing anything now?" asked the lawyer.

"Yes," said Ben. "I'm writing about civil war."

"Ooh," cooed Jill. "How so?"

"You mean, *how* am I writing it, or…"

"I mean, what inspires you?"

"Our country, probably, or the French Revolution."

"What do you mean, 'our country'?" asked the lawyer.

"America?"

"Oh," said Jill, confused. "But we're not *in* a civil war."

"In a way, we are," said Ben. "We just pretend we're not."

"Oh listen to this…" Jill laughed.

Ben, however, did not seem discouraged, and continued.

"Red state, blue state. Us, them. Black, white, legal, illegal. Religious rights, human rights. Guns, no guns. I mean, we may not be out-and-out shooting at each other, like in a movie, but it is a war."

"Has he seen our adorable little hero at the Watsons, Nancy?" asked Jill.

"No, he hasn't, Jill."

"Well, we've absolutely got to take him. Speaking of which, where are the Watsons?"

"They didn't make it," said Mark, and Jill didn't seem upset by this, nor did she seem to gather the nuances of their lack of attendance.

The lawyer looked at Ben.

"What's wrong with guns, son?" He wolfed down a carrot stick.

"Plenty of things," ventured Ben. "Regardless, I own one."

"You own a gun?" shouted Nancy, a bit embarrassed at her tone.

Ben just looked at her.

"Yes, I own a gun," he said, and it was the first time she heard a note of annoyance in his voice. She caught, briefly, a glimmer in his eye, and considered that he might be lying to them, something to press their buttons, these bitter, old reactionaries. She couldn't decide, but she was mildly ashamed at her response to him and tried to compensate by offering him some peacock cake. He said no without looking at her.

Jill's lawyer groaned something about predictability, stereotypes, liberals, and social justice, which is when Ben looked at his phone, and found an empty table.

Nancy didn't blame him. It was enough to drive across the country, but to have a pit-stop at your aunt's house and meet with this group only exacerbated the awkwardness of the situation.

"There's no damn culture war; everything is splendid. Better than ever, in fact," said Jill's lawyer, but people had stopped listening, and Jill was gathering a last minute group to go up and see the peacock. She managed to corral Nancy and Ben, but not Kevin, who said he'd see them at home. A few mothers and their children went along with them. Once they got to the top of the hill and parked on the Watson's property, Jill ushered everyone over to the fence, where the sign —Nancy was stunned to see—remained in the ground exactly where Jill had left it. Even Jill appeared pleased by this, as if the Watsons were in agreement with her, after all.

"Everyone gather close," said Jill.

She used a mini-flashlight key-chain to guide everyone over to the fence. The night was darker than usual; Nancy had a private moment of panic that her eyesight might be going, and why was the Watson property so dark? No trigger lights, nothing.

"Okay everyone!" Jill stuck the flashlight through the fence and waved it around, trying to land on the peacock, but only caught the dread-filled eyes of the other animals who had been sleeping up to this point. Now they faced Jill and her maniacal light.

"Here, beautiful thing! Here!" She called to it, but nothing came; then, waltzing toward the back of the pen was the peacock.

"There! There! Look! Look now!" She screeched, and everyone pressed forward. Ben—hands shoved into his pockets—saw the bird, then casually went back to the car. His face was colder, Nancy noticed, as if he was making a decision, and wanted to be away from everyone.

"Here, dearhreart! Here!" Jill's howl escalated.

Floodlights along the roof of the Watson's house shot on and the entire pen lit-up. Confused by the sudden glare, each animal stood or ran to hide in nearby corners. Mr. Watson, shotgun in hand, came around the yard. He had the look of someone jolted out of sleep. The expression of annoyance, disappointment, and disbelief was unmistakable, even in the night.

"Get off my property, show's over."

"But, Mr. Watson, I just wanted to show these people my amazing bird."

"It's not *your* bird, and it's not the neighborhood

bird. Now, we're trying to sleep. You can either get off my land, or I'll kick you off it. Your choice."

"Let's go, guys," said Jill. "Clearly, Mr. Watson's not a team player. Clearly, he's too good for us."

"Go on, let's go, get out of here," said Mr. Watson. He stood there and waited until we left before he walked back inside, and the flood lights shut off.

Back at home, Ben politely excused himself, and went to bed. Nancy did the same thing, trying to push away an image of Jill—silent, unblinking, and red-faced— driving them back. The next day, they all stayed in, and the following morning, Ben left. Nancy had shown him to the door and wished him a safe drive, and apologized for "the awkwardness." She noticed he didn't seem to care. She shut the door and went back to sleep. Nancy had already seen the peacock on her roof once at 6:00 AM, and it was there again, while she slept, the fields still dark. It hopped to the ground, then made its way down the road to the next neighboring property. It held a circuitous route, as if it just wanted to take in a quick walk before it got back to the Watson's farm. It was there, on its strange u-turn heading back in the direction from which it came, that the bullet found him, a quick pop that echoed into the still air on the empty road; the shot was followed by a weak, pathetic squawk from its throat. Neither Nancy nor Kevin heard it, and even Mr. Watson, asleep in a chair in his living room, wasn't privy to the final act, the clean, singular burst of sound, just down the road. Only one of the neighbors heard it.

Because the peacock was found dead on Nancy's front lawn, Jill did not hesitate to confront her in public at the market in the closest town where they all did their shopping. Jill got her attention by slapping Nancy across her right cheek as she examined a jar of pickled herring.

"You fuckin' bitch," she said, spitting onto her chin. "You shot God's Glorious Splendor!"

"Go home, Jill," was all Nancy could manage.

When Nancy got to the parking lot, her tires had been slashed. She called Kevin, and the car was towed to a garage somewhere in town.

"If it wasn't you that killed it," wrote Jill in an email to Nancy, "then it was that lib-tard, gay-flame nephew of yours."

Nancy blocked her email; Jill blocked Nancy on social media. Kevin said he felt like he was being followed home from work one day, and then later, after leaving the gym. Nancy suggested they call the police and file a report, but Kevin refused. A week later, Nancy's car was spray-painted with a slogan that read: "My gay-tard nephew killed God's Glorious Splendor!"

The police told her she would need proof Jill had done it before charges could be brought. By the end of the year, the Watsons had sold their farm and moved to Montana. No one knew for months. Kevin left for the gym one day at his regular time without a word, and never returned, texting Nancy later that he planned to move to the city, and to stay there. By April, Jill had divorced Mark and moved to Florida, where her mother lived. The other neighbors, south of Nancy, were too distant to make any kind of regular connection. She'd only met them twice, and at Jill's cookouts, and so didn't reserve any kind of hope that they'd become friends.

The following December, she received a call from Ben, asking if he could stay with her again on his way home for the winter break. She said of course, and asked him when he'd arrive, so she could prepare a room for him. Ben inquired about the neighbors.

"You won't have to worry about any of them. Drive safely, and I'll see you when you get here. Call from the road if you need anything."

"I will," he said.

The house was quiet lately, even more than when Kevin lived there, yet was gone all of the time. Nancy preferred this kind of silence; she recognized herself in it. She thought of it as a gift to herself, and she began to find ways to give herself more gifts. Back in October, she found something nestled in the weeds of her yard. A single, green peacock feather broken in the middle, mauled by its time tossed around in the elements. Holding it between thumb and forefinger as if it might disintegrate, she gently brushed it with her fingertips. She took it inside and wrapped it in a piece of thin tissue paper, and put it in a drawer with a few other things she hoped to forget one day, but never did.

CONSUMMATION

Mariabelle followed a mother and her daughter at the lion exhibit. Other than the three of them, the exhibit was deserted. She kept her distance while the mother and daughter stood at the gate, peeking over the railing at the large male stretched out on the grass, eyes blinking sleepily in the sun. Its tail lifted and fell behind it, his massive head turning occasionally, indifferent to the two of them standing there.

The woman held her young daughter up in her arms so she could see. Her black hair stopped at her jaw, obscuring her face, and the daughter's tiny arm stretched out, pointing. The mother nodded to something she said. The girl's navy blue coat was shaped like a bell, and it spread out around her when the mother lowered her back to the ground. Mariabelle assessed the woman's long gray overcoat, black pumps, and black stockings. She envied her large black sunglasses and hungered to have the same kind of poise the woman held. She didn't want to be caught staring, so she looked away for a minute. When she looked back, the two had moved further down from her, still close to the railing. The child dropped her stuffed toy through the bars, and the mother bent down to say something to the girl. The little girl screamed, then calmed, and Mariabelle heard the woman raise her voice in a reassuring tone, repeating that it was okay.

She lifted the child up again and helped her climb over the railing to the den, catching the fleeting attention of the lions. The woman's tone rose. *You're fine. You're fine, honey, go on, get your toy.* The girl clasped the edge of the railing, looking behind her then back to her mother, her wet face crinkled into uncertainty, which dissipated into a kind of focus as she climbed down the other side, trusting that her mother was correct about this. Once the child vanished behind the railing, the woman walked away.

•

Mariabelle told no one what she saw at the zoo. She did nothing. She just stared at the woman's back until she disappeared near one of the gazebos, swallowed in a crowd of ambling patrons. Awe filled her and the icy minutiae of the fall day gained razor crispness. She held onto this feeling. She chose the opposite direction and walked away from the exhibit. In that instant, she and the mother were the same person, and she wondered what, if anything, the mother felt when she left. Mariabelle tried to affect a similar posture that exuded the exact confidence seen under the woman's long, gray coat.

She kept this moment to herself, rare and furtive, like something endangered held in her palm.

•

Mariabelle sat at a Coffee Bean & Tea Leaf eating a muffin. The barista brought it to her on a tiny ceramic plate with a small silver fork. She tucked into herself. Her left arm draped over her stomach as if to hold it in place, and she leaned at a diagonal over the table. Her narrow, oval face expressed compacted aggravation, annoyance that she had to eat anything, but that her body demanded it, which was already malnourished, waif-like, despite the occasional nights of taco binging and pizzas.

Her tissue-thin, mocha-brown cardigan hung on the knobs of her shoulders, open to the mauve button-top blouse with a lace collar. It stopped at the bony hip of her plain black skirt. She wore black stockings over her blanched legs. Pleated slippers covered her flat feet. She kept her brown hair smooth between her shoulders and her bangs set in a severe line across her forehead, even though it was a style that was fading. Mariabelle's black, vintage, cat-styled eye glasses were a bit wide for her face, but she bought them for this reason, as if to draw attention to the style of the glasses, and not her oily nose, or the undefined landscape of her face, which could be described, tentatively, as unremarkable, and she had heard it put in such terms before when people didn't think she was listening. Her affected demureness verged on mouse-like: her hunched-in quality, the bony hands, and the continuance of her post-graduate, quasi-French New Wave aesthetic. She knew many girls had achieved a similar look readily lumping them within an accessible bracket and identity; she had, in part, adopted it from them, but methodically curated her own take on it long before she matriculated to Columbia. Incisive, she had marinated in these reductive choices from the corner bedroom of her parents' Park Slope brownstone.

Mariabelle drove the tiny fork into the mottled crown of the muffin and peck-peck-pecked at the chunk, almost dropping it. Her face and jaw jolted as if she had to hurry and get it in, like a starving bird snapping at crumbs under a table. Her cheeks reddened from an embarrassed awareness of the wide motions of her chewing. When she finished, she slumped like someone who just endured something very unnecessary and unspeakable as if the muffin had been indignant toward her.

She stood up and left, walking down the street back to her office, head lowered with a slight undertone of false modesty. A block away from the teashop she entered an office building and took an elevator to the fourth floor, which housed *Non*, the literary journal and publishing house for which she'd been an acquisitions editor for the last two years.

Her workspace consisted of a small desk in a corner near the editor-in-chief's office, and had no real walls or demarcations, just a desk and a computer where many had sat before her. She put her tiny brown purse on the floor and pulled forward in her chair, clicking computer keys. Most of the staff worked with exhausted focus, consumed by their own editorial duties. Craig, an intern from NYU, often initiated slim efforts to converse with her, prompted, she guessed, by his need for approval. His forthright kindness toward her made her squeamish, and this time he began small talk that caused her to look away. He smirked, moved back a bit, and said, "You know, you're like royalty being told to wait in front of that thing."

She sat up, confused by his tone. He pointed at her desktop. "The computer," he said with a flattened mouth, and left.

•

It was her lack of sexuality that motivated most of her choices. She was tepid and many men never looked at her bird-like frame as a sexual opportunity. Her penchant during her college years to include a thread of adolescence in her womanhood only served to heighten the nerd-aesthetic she worked so thoroughly to appear muted now, at 24, while at the same time distinct, a conundrum that often drove men to other, more assertive women; she struggled against this, endeavoring to germinate some kind of sexual appeal and ended up relegated to the margins. The men that her body starved for with entrenched biological insistence were almost overtly masculine, usually blond, athletic in some way, and indifferent to her. Affecting any form of lofty cuteness around them as a post-graduate always provoked visible wilting in their bodies. They became slack. Their muscularity shrank somehow, and the conversations became quick, shallow, dismissive.

●

Her relationship with Auden began when she left Columbia and started working for *Non*. Her friend, Ava, who worked in the law firm adjacent to Auden's, facilitated their meeting at a function held at the MoMA, after which Ava insisted that they go back to her Village apartment to have some "go-powder," and look at the Kandinsky she just inherited from her grandmother. Ava, like other girls Mariabelle knew from Columbia, began similarly: the same wealth-aloofness sticking to her like the strings of black hair on the back of her neck, unavoidable, permanent. But Ava had eradicated the fictile, ersatz comeliness, trading it for a law firm severity, or finessed-business-privilege. Mariabelle moved with her standard foot dragging, trying to upstage Ava's refined unapproachability with her own, then losing it when Auden continued to talk to her with a kind of interest she'd never before experienced.

He had the athletic body she desired, but it was trimmed down, and his hair was brown instead of blond. He seemed not to see any of her the way that she saw herself; he leaned toward her when she spoke, he listened, and his body seemed to open up. He put his hand on top of hers, a shell cupping a shell. She tried not to acknowledge this. It was unexpected, but the warmth and pressure of his fingers expressed a measure of solidity. This allowed Mariabelle to lessen her original slanted posture wrapped snug in the brown cardigan when they took turns snorting Ava's "go-powder" under her new Kandinsky.

A challenge arose between them, an unspoken contest between her and Ava to appear the most unaffected by the amount they just inhaled. Auden, sitting with one leg hanging over the arm of his chair, wore white pants that revealed nothing of his muscularity. He talked about boats and how he intended to get one. He sipped at a glass of soda water with a bright lemon sliver shoved into the ice.

"My grandfather has two. My dad has two. I have none. The races for these things are tight. My dad says they usually determine partnership in most cases."

"What about speedboats?" asked Ava, looking away from him to her phone.

"I've never been on a boat," Mariabelle offered, pulling her knees closer to her on the couch.

"Yachts are dumb," said Auden. "I'm interested in regattas, but no yachts. Power vessels. Ships that divide water like a clean blade."

"I want sushi," whined Ava.

When Ava fell asleep under her coffee table around 5:00 AM, Auden kept his attention on Mariabelle, talking for hours about boating and merits, his rise up the ranks, and she thought about herself, how when Paul Auster once came to the magazine to do a personal interview, she was allowed to sit in and take notes. Later, on her resume, she wrote: *Writing Workshop with Paul Auster at Non: A Literary Journal, Spring 2014 - NYC.* She did the same thing with Donna Tartt, and later turned every work meeting into a writing conference. The meritocracy was important to Mariabelle, too. She just kept her accomplishments quieter than others.

•

At the same time that she began seeing Auden regularly, she started a band with two neighbors in her building called *Lies Mold Soft Minds*. Jones and Katharine lived together. Jones's mother and father were known actors and Mariabelle could remember staying up with her dad during summer nights watching films that starred them. Katherine wasn't subtle about Jones's upbringing, explaining that Jones is only interested in living "authentically," so asked for very little help from his famous parents. Katherine suggested the band while she shared an American Spirit with Mariabelle in the hallway of their mutual floor. A spiral staircase with an old wooden railing divided it, leading from the building's entrance to the roof.

"The landlord doesn't care," said Katherine, passing the cigarette to Mariabelle. "As long as we don't do it in our apartments, or on the fire-escape. I don't know why."

They sat with their legs through the posts of the railing, swinging their feet. Katherine wore acid-washed denim. Her hair was shaved up one side with feathers braided into the sheaf falling down the other side of her pale face. She left and came back with a blue, toy keyboard, and a scratched, purple banjo, and both started pounding on them with what was an informed irony at first, which eventually unspooled into a contemplative seriousness they negotiated in silence while they made up a song together. Jones stood watching in the open door, a wide-billed hat propped on his head, mustache blending into unshaven cheeks, black t-shirt and beige cut-off shorts, a perspiring PBR in his hand.

"You guys sound like Cat Power fucked Cat Power."

"At least we're original, you fuck," said Katherine, implicating his choice in clothes and laughing smoke out of her nostrils.

They stopped their improvisation when Auden came up the stairs. Mariabelle dropped the toy piano, and went to him where he stood at her door. She introduced him to Jones and Katherine, telling him they had just formed a band. He appeared oddly exuberant, eager to support her. Each group went back to their separate apartments, and that night Auden proposed.

•

Mariabelle began to attribute all of the successes in her life to the possible death of the child at the zoo. Her practices with Jones and Katherine every week increased in quality, it seemed, and they played their first show at a bar in Alphabet City, which was attended by a large crowd Mariabelle accredited to the appearance of Jones's parents, sitting coldly in the first row. Both had withered fatigue in their faces as if their actor selves were other bodies they slipped on when required. Mariabelle played her toy keyboard and Katherine sang in a voice like syrup over the insistent plucking of Jones's fingers on the purple banjo. His two parents nodded in tandem, approval and duty in one gesture.

Auden stood in back by the bar drinking a beer and clapped with genuine appreciation and support. This lifted something in Mariabelle. After they finished playing, she curled into him, once again a little girl, his arm snug around her, congratulating her on the first performance. Jones walked up later with Katherine at his side.

"*Lies Mold Soft Minds!*" Someone shouted gutturally from the crowd. Jones jumped, turning around to scan the audience, and Mariabelle thought he looked panicked, vulnerable, and exposed somehow. He drank his beer with shaky hands and wide eyes.

After the show, Auden and Mariabelle returned to her apartment. When Auden held her post-sex, naked and sweaty, she thought his hands always signaled too much plainspoken intent, but she didn't mind. She was sore because it took him so long. He looked at her with an expression intimating a vague need for feedback, or possibly reassurance. Compared to him, her body was a length of sketched bone pulled taut under her white skin. They talked about the marriage and how it would be, who would appear, and what they would do afterward. Then, Auden brought up secrets.

"What are yours?"

Mariabelle wanted to tell him about the zoo, but that was sacrosanct, so she made up something about always wanting to have sex in a library, something she never thought of doing, but it was lukewarm, passable.

"Can I tell you mine?" said Auden, not waiting for her response as if he had started this game for the purposes of this alone.

"Well," he said, "I sometimes like the guys."

"What does that mean? 'The guys'," she asked.

"It just means sometimes I like the guys."

•

That week Mariabelle had lunch at her mother's insistence, demanding that she come to their brownstone in Park Slope. Mariabelle slumped in the white metal chair and both of them had salads with salmon slices layered across the plates in pink slabs. Mariabelle stared at the plate in her large brown sunglasses, one knee up in the chair, one arm dangling.

"Oh honey, you've got to eat something…and don't sit like that."

Mariabelle took a bite of fish and swallowed it.

"You can't worry about this. Don't marry the gay ones. Don't do that to yourself, or you'll never be satisfied."

"He's not."

"Closet cases are like Republicans, darling, they only make sense to themselves."

How could Mariabelle explain to her mother what she already knew to be true about her position, which was that if Auden wanted to marry her, and she had to accept his love for men as a part of the deal, then it was better than the inevitable nothing that waited for her otherwise.

She watched her mother's hands, the gloss of her

manicure, and the practiced poise of her fingers as she spread golden fig jam across a piece of Melba toast. Silver and diamonds sprouted from her knuckles like crustaceans.

"Marry up, Maria! Marry up! If you don't get what you want, you *bully* your way there. That's what successful people do; they bully their way to what they want. Look at us!"

There are other ways, too, she thought.

"You still want to publish something, don't you? Well, then bully your way to it. Don't wait around to be recognized. You think anyone's getting anywhere anymore by doing things the polite way? The old fashioned way? And what's with this band? Auden's a fine man, honey, but you're never going to be satisfied."

●

At night, Mariabelle searched the Internet for news regarding the little girl at the zoo. Acute anxiety caused her heart to flip-flop in a frightening drop of pressure when she thought there might be nothing; that all of this wealth in her life could be lost very easily if nothing corroborated the girl's death. She looked everywhere, combed databases, searched articles, and once came close to calling the zoo to ask if they ever found the girl. Her hands were numb and her head tight from the tension of scrutinizing every article she came across. She found both multiple missing children cases and a stream of other horrors, hundreds: kids found dead in fields, frozen to the ground states away from their homes. Children flung out of rollercoaster carts; some left in cars overnight and found days later by passing strangers; a boy tied to a post in a garage and force-fed dog food; two sisters mutilated in a house fire when their father left space heaters on next to the curtains, then went gambling with his girlfriend; another boy drowned in a pool, but the parents hadn't noticed for three days since they had been fighting all weekend. One woman in New Jersey ran over her own baby. She told the officers later that she forgot to put it in the car, but when she left she just kept going, not caring what she'd done.

Mariabelle found nothing about the girl, nothing that described a child being devoured by a lion, or anything about blood showered on a stone, or screaming onlookers. There was nothing about a mother who had fed her child to the beasts below. Nothing at all. But then she did find something. A single article that described everything she had seen. They were looking for a woman (the mother?), who had been in charge of this child, and they were looking for the child. Apparently someone else witnessed what the woman had done, another watcher, although there was no mention of any other witnesses. The child was simply reported as "missing," but that did not, Mariabelle told herself, mean the same thing as "unconsumed." It was this thought, finally, that gave Mariabelle unexpected relief, and she shut off her computer.

•

Auden started to seem withdrawn and Mariabelle couldn't figure out why. His odd silences went unexamined. She began to wonder if he doubted their relationship, now, or if it was something else; that maybe he began to perceive what their commitment really meant, who he would become when it was final. As the wedding date approached, Mariabelle knew she would need to return to the zoo. She hoped there would be a finite indication of the child's death, a clue perhaps. It took her days to find some courage to ask Auden to join her because she knew he would want to know why, and because it was a place no one would ever suspect her of visiting for the purposes of her own solitude. She

wanted Auden along for the journey because she needed someone else to see where it happened; she wasn't
entirely sure why this was important to her. Becoming
the kinds of people she imagined they would become
was an alchemy, she knew, that was somehow contin-
gent upon a visitation, and whatever it revealed; their
greater selves were at stake, the *future* them. They did
care for one another; it was inevitable in some ways,
but moreover, it was herself at whom she was surprised,
burdened by this new shock that she was capable of
any such feeling. So when she finally asked Auden to
go with her, he agreed rather companionably. To her
relief, the most he offered to her random request was a
surprised lift of his dark eyebrows.

The day's brightness filtered itself through an abrupt
cold front when nature began its incremental turn. Un-
derscoring this was an icy wind that smelled of metal.
Mariabelle had lost much of her reserved pomposity by
now, so that when she walked arm-in-arm with Auden,
there was an actual legitimate confidence to it. They arrived at the lion exhibit, which was sparsely populated,
as it was the last time she had come. An elderly couple
walked behind them, pacified into dopey smiles by the
weather. The trees around them shifted in a cold clat-
tering of leaves, then silence. Mariabelle experienced

an electric shift in her abdomen when she saw the gate, the exact spot where the woman and girl had stood. She recalled the mother's black hair, and the girl's bell-shaped coat.

"What made you want to come here?" asked Auden, waiting.

There was a moment where neither said anything, and she wasn't sure she could answer him. He seemed to want a genuine response, now. He insinuated as much. What would happen if she gave it to him? How would things be different once they left the zoo? She looked at him.

"Just something I thought you should see, Auden." Her voice was softer and calmer than she expected. She wanted that to suffice, to end it, but was unable to tell if it did. Something in her went hollow. Silence took hold of them again as they watched the grass in the exhibit, the jolts and tugs of it in the wind.

Out toward the distance, their gazes drifted, no longer aware that they looked together. Hypnotized, they saw some shadow-movement in the bracken, and they waited while it came to find them where they stood.

ACE OF SWORDS

While no one was around, Jeremiah Felton considered what he'd done with the birds. He thought that loneliness killed, and he wasn't incorrect. He was attempting to follow this thought, which arose so quietly while he sat at his desk. His office had a seventh story view of the sunbaked, 4WARD-Com parking lot. Jim, his co-worker, parked his hunter-green Subaru in the third row by itself. The brown Jeep one row up was Mary's, the Office Manager next door to him, and he could even spot her daughter's piggy-corn stuffed animal (a mutation that crosses a pig and a unicorn together), lying across the front seat, one limp arm dangling over its edge as if wilted by the heat coming in through the car's windows.

This idea about loneliness bloomed through an unforeseen interstice not normally permitted in Jeremiah's office, and it took him away from his computer, his desk, his space, forcing him to observe, arbitrarily, the state of the building's parking lot. The sounds of the office were predictable and consistent, including the chemical, electronic jingle of his Outlook in-box; every pre-programmed, vibrating ringtone on his cell phone; the numb, assiduous clicking of the secretaries on their keyboards in the outer office at the reception desk, a hulking parenthesis constructed out of deep-burgundy wood and black marble. The sign for his lending company, Titul-AR Finance, (small businesses, small home loans, full mortgages), was stamped on the front in silver copperplate. Although the company was housed in the 4WARD-Com building, it had its own wing.

Jeremiah tried to trace his thought on loneliness to its origins, to understand it the way one might try to trace one's indigestion back to what had been eaten, negotiating a mild disbelief that anything that had been consumed would have such a disruptive effect on the system and, at last, ignoring it once it had passed. The thought gained a kind of ethereal quality the harder he pushed at it, trying to hold onto the strange notion it offered, creating a sudden and violent contrast within his office. He became momentarily repulsed by it, a place of multiple handshakes and congratulations, smoldering talks concerning what he felt had become a country of Takers; the loss of faith in the joys of trickle-down economics, and boy's baseball (a team was begun by Mary's husband, Francis, for the sons of the members of Titul-AR Finance; and games often tied into the annual pot-luck and lamb roast), another pastime attacked by what he called the politically correct nut-jobs moving into their neighborhoods, accusing them of subjecting children to fascism when Francis ordered uniforms in all red with the team name, *RepubliCANS!* scrawled across them in white (the manufacturer suggested blue lettering for contrast, but Francis became angry, stating that blue was for the *other* side, and would be an affront to the meaning behind the uniforms). The children, however, never asked what the name meant, and most wanted them off the minute the games ended, covered as they were in spilled Gatorade, mud, and sometimes vomit if one of them ate beforehand.

Leslie, one of the administrators behind the reception desk, tapped on Jeremiah's door, and pulled his attention away from the scorched cars in the parking lot.

"Mr. Felton? It's time."

"Thank you, Leslie."

She departed with a sensual, yet professional twist to her hips as she walked back to the reception area. Jeremiah stood from his desk, shelving his thoughts on loneliness, and left his office to meet the other members congregating in the larger conference room. Men and women in black blazers and navy-blue pantsuits stood in clusters. Black leather chairs leaned out from a massive mahogany table in the center. Pitchers of water stood in ellipsis, and each seat had its own unused yellow legal pad, a new pen, and an empty glass for the water. Most of it would not be used. The glasses would stay empty, and the water would be poured out later. Leslie would have one of the underlings collect most of the remaining legal pads, and everyone would pocket the pens. After some general, surface conversation with others in various groups around the room, Clyde, the president of Titul-AR Finance, began his customary ceremonies.

"Everyone gather hands," he said, his low-voice like gravel strained through a vice.

Jeremiah grasped hands with Pauline and Samuel.

Pauline was a twenty-year veteran of the company, and Samuel just graduated from the state university. Pauline's grasp communicated a kind of resigned duty, whereas Samuel's suggested a lack of surety, a naïve hopefulness in the forthright way he clasped Jeremiah's palm; he seemed vaguely uncomfortable with what they were doing here in the conference room every Wednesday.

"Everyone bow," said Clyde. "Lord, we thank you for this bounty. The bounty you have given us. For the upswing in numbers this last fall, to the record breaking numbers in the last year. We pray today, the way we pray every day; that you continue to bring us this bounty, as we continue to praise you. Amen."

"Amen."

During the meeting Pauline took them through her slow and terse PowerPoint. Afterwards, Clyde congratulated those who had contributed the most to the "record breaking numbers," of which Jeremiah was one of them.

"And Mr. Felton," said Clyde. "What a job you have done. What a job. Look at you bringing it home this last quarter. Aren't we impressed, Ladies and Gentlemen?"

Applause ricocheted around the room.

Jeremiah's department was responsible for repossessions. He divided up the phone calls with a colleague, and they earned a percentage, or fee, on the foreclosures. During the phone calls, the screaming sounds of outraged families poured through the receiver; men came close to coronaries as they showered Jeremiah in expletives; mothers sobbed that their home was being taken from them; children in the background sometimes cried, or pleaded to know what was wrong with their parents, who couldn't stop the torrent racing from their mouths into Jeremiah's ear.

Jeremiah listened to all of them, and when there was a gap, or opportunity, he wedged himself into the cacophony, and said, "I understand you're upset. Due to failure to pay, your home has been repossessed and is in foreclosure. You have twenty-four hours to vacate the property. Anything left on the property will be disposed of by the city. Thank you for being a part of Tit-ul-AR Finance," and he hung up.

"A genius," said Clyde, who bragged of the record amount of foreclosures Jeremiah had managed in the last year alone. "And tell me again, what did that last woman say? The one whose husband shot himself. She ended up living out of a hotel, I think, with her poor son, who's missing, now. Absolute negligence, if you ask me."

Jeremiah looked around the room.

"She said I make my living off of the suffering and misfortunes of others."

"Isn't that a wonder? What balls, if I can say it outright? Just thoughtless. You've done a great job," said Clyde, and the room listened eagerly as he redirected the conversation to numbers again, and then closed the meeting with another prayer.

On the way back to his office, Leslie gave him a congratulatory wink. He sat down in his chair and looked out of his window. Jim's Subaru was gone, as was Mary's Jeep. The parking lot glimmered in the heat. Jeremiah didn't understand why there was such emptiness to it, or why he felt it should be filled, or even why it mattered.

He wanted to remember his original thought, and he couldn't.

Leaving the 4WARD-Com building, snug in his warm Audi, Jeremiah drove north on the freeway to the pet store before it closed. He bought six finches. It was all they had besides parakeets, and it was time for a change. He got a cheap cage to carry them in, hesitant to overspend since he would just throw it away like all of the others once he got home and put the birds to use.

Neetch worm (*Nosconasiosis)* is a tubular parasite that grows in the creek beds formed by drainage and sewage runoff. Born feeding on the bacteria in fecal matter, or fermented garbage, the parasite develops a shape like a bloated centipede with a pale, gray body that modulates and contorts using a singular muscular system. If left to develop over time it grows a spine that resembles the branch of a pine tree, the spinal column being the central rod around which multiple bone-needles reach from end-to-end. The speculation is that it is a kind of defense against potential predators that might decide to bite into its soft body, only to sink teeth into a thorny interior. Neetch worms are hermaphroditic and inseminate themselves when they've acquired enough girth to carry a birth sack, a thick blister-like coagulant that forms on its back near the head. Usually reaching the maximum size of a child's forearm, *Nosconasiosis* no longer has the strength or adaptive elements (hunting) to find nutrients, and instead lays a scent trap for other mammals, including deer, rabbits, and domestic animals. It attaches itself to the victim with rounded, blunt teeth that are both found on the top and bottom of the main orifice, or 'throat', since it lacks a full mouth. Once attached, it uses its muscular system to propel a syringe-tongue upwards. Its saliva, containing a numbing acid, eats through the tougher parts of dermal layers over a course of about a few hours, allowing the tongue to burst through easily; it searches for a central vein, or artery, and the process of draining its host is slow. Tiny slits open along the walls of the interior of the throat, where the tongue deposits the host's serum for absorption into its body.

Nosconasiosis can live up to six years, and perhaps longer if supplied with a steady food surplus. The oldest recorded living *Nosconasiosis* (10 years), grew a series of eyes along its back that resembled black acne, the most prominent of which had a yellow iris, and an odd smiling expression; in common parlance among parasitologists it is referred to as the "Grinner." The parasite is only found in North America, where it is believed to have originated and evolved.

•

Jeremiah didn't want to do it today, but he did it anyway. He went through the kitchen so no one would see him, especially his wife, and opened the door to the stairs leading to the basement. The birds chirped in their awkward, white metal cage as he took the steps cautiously. A light had been left on down here, and he chided himself, thinking of the fires it could have caused, and of all the other potential problems. A single bulb without a shade dangled over a sanded door he had been working on. It lay flat across a workbench. He took a seat on his small, wooden stool, placing the cage with the birds in front of him on the sanded door. The cage came with a white, canvas cloak, which he pulled off like a sock, and watched the tiny, round finches jostle and jump, peeking up at him, chirping, trying to get a grasp on their new environment.

Jeremiah dragged the cage closer and watched them for some time. At a certain point they became still, and he wondered if they were frightened. He had seed down here from the birds he had kept before, and went to get some, returning to sprinkle a mix through the bars of the cage. He went upstairs and came back with water, which he poured into the birds' drinking bowl. One hopped toward the bowl, drinking without reluctance. Watching this caused something to open up in Jeremiah and, for a moment, he was overwhelmed by their cuteness, if that's what you could call it. This softening—a tangible, liquid parting of the tension throughout his body—was why he did it; or, this was the first, *paramount* reason, whereas the other reasons were more convoluted and untraceable. There were things he needed and wanted, but a barrier existed preventing him from knowing what those things were. He gathered, in part, that this barrier existed because of his choices from working at the finance company, and he understood what its nature really entailed. He wasn't completely naïve about it. How could he be? But Vickie, his wife, was happy, and his son and daughters were as well. Jeremiah was not only able to purchase a vacation condo in Jupiter, Florida from the recent foreclosures he accomplished alone, but he was also able to buy his son (newly eleven), a Jet Ski. With his eldest daughter, Julie, at college, he had little to worry about when it came to spending anything extra on her. His wife wept when he'd told her about the commissions, clinging to him in their bathroom once they'd put Jonathan to bed.

"My God, the *tile*. Just think about what I'll be able to do with the *tile* to that place! My God, I'm so excited!"

Everything they had was the direct result of the work he did: their homes, their cars, all of it. There was a period of pride, where he beamed at what he'd built, which faded and was replaced by something far more hollow, a reverberation he mistook for an age-related crisis. So overcome by it, he'd ended up in the emergency room twice during the year, convinced he was having a heart attack, yet discovered after multiple tests, that it was just plain panic. Searching for an explanation for this sudden vacuity, where once there was an almost lurid fullness provided by the material wealth he and Vickie had accrued (including the incredible numbers in his bank account), he had very little by way of an answer. What was happening—both at work and at home—did not reflect back to him the identity he was given during his upbringing in Texas. But the hollowness was still there, and nothing in his job or his family showed the opposite; the gravity of this transcended a simple lack of fulfillment, or depression. The hollow was so large that he couldn't see himself outside of it at all.

Jeremiah adjusted the cage over the rough patches of the sanded door, and brought his face close to it, observing the curious, perky indifference of the animals inside. He caught the eye of one, its head tilted. He spoke to it softly, like he would to a baby, quoting Pascal as he had done many times before: *Dividing these last things again, let him exhaust his powers of conception...Perhaps he will think that here is the smallest point in nature. I will let him see therein a new abyss. I will paint for him not only the visible universe, but all that he can conceive of nature's immensity in the womb of this abridged atom.* The bird hopped over to the seed and began to eat. Some of them remained still, peering beyond their cage to something else. Occasionally one would twist its head and burrow its beak into the feathers of its wing and fluff itself.

Jeremiah's back started to ache the longer he sat on the stool, and he knew it was time to get going because Vickie would want dinner soon, and his son would want him to watch as he shot people on his video game. He stood and walked past the pile of other cages he had yet to throw out, and which went unseen and unquestioned by Vickie (she stayed in the world above, like he asked). He went toward the back of the room to the corner where he had his walk-in safe, which came complete with a light inside, and he had a TV monitor rigged to the top right corner of one of its shelves.

The light flickered on when he opened the door, like a refrigerator, and the smell was less strong this time; more like old coffee and soaked mulch, dirt, or rotting tree bark. Careful not to kick or step upon any of the small bird bodies in piles on the floor, he leaned up to the TV monitor and flipped the switch. A blue screen glowed over the piled shapes, and one or two on the shelves. Outside of the safe was a DVD player. Jeremiah went to slide in a disk and press play. The scene that came on the screen offered the crisp sounds of a wet jungle during a light summer shower. There were bird-calls and other animal sounds.

The echo of it coming from the safe across the rest of the basement made him think for a moment that it could pass as a doorway into another realm; that, if you let yourself believe in it for a minute, it really was an-other place, a portal, a direct opening into something inexplicable and maybe even labyrinthine. At times, he thought of locking himself in there with the birds, and waiting to see if a door did open, like the stories he'd read as a boy. It seemed so many of them professed that there were portals everywhere, you just had to look in the right spot; and, more than that, there were other universes. Jeremiah never knew which was more ex-citing to him when he read the stories: the portal, the discovery of the portal, or what the portal led to.

For a minute, he focused on the back wall of the safe, and something moved. He saw it. The wall became like a black pool, and then something came closer, something reflected back. It was large and had multiple faces, eyes that sought out food of some kind. He could see its legs, its mouths. And then it shook itself back into the dark. A light began somewhere in the moving liquid, purple light, and it started to reveal a land of some sort. He could see it. The outline of it was there. A valley of some kind. Homes.

With the TV monitor playing its rainforest jungle scenes, Jeremiah lifted the cage and took it inside the safe. He squatted down, still maintaining a close eye on where he put his feet—the space was sacred. The smell didn't bother him, and neither did the medium-sized pyramids of bird corpses, but the sound of their tiny bones popping underneath his work shoes would cause him to crumble. And he didn't want to know what that would do. He treated them like explosives, attributing them with danger to keep himself from taking his footing for granted.

Placing the cage between his legs, he leaned out and grabbed the handle to the door of the safe, then he put a wooden mop handle between the door and the jamb to block the door from closing completely and locking him inside. He lifted the tiny sliding hatch of the white cage, separating the cage from its base. The top parted smoothly, and the birds scattered, some flying up to the shelves. Others perched on the wilted bodies of diamond doves and zebra finches decomposing in the corners, and then flew to higher places.

It took a few minutes, but he was finally able to grab one. He held it gently in his hands, taking note of its lightness, the severe lightness of its feathers. The bird tilted its head, looking around and up at Jeremiah. It didn't peck or claw, but just seemed to accept its place in his hands like it did the cage. The others had grown still again at the back of the safe, a few huddled close to one another, and one stayed on top of the heap of bones and feathers.

Jeremiah crawled out fast and closed the safe door, sealing the birds inside it. He wouldn't return for another month, perhaps, and with a new cage and new birds. He turned off the light to the basement and went up, entering into the bright kitchen. In the living room, his son indeed played one of his games.

Jeremiah stood there for a moment, observing how his son jumped around as he navigated an animated figure across a desert terrain, shooting other figures into sprays of red. His son turned around when he realized someone stood behind him.

"How's it going, son?"

"Good," he said, pausing his game. He looked at his dad with a modicum of irritation. Jeremiah realized

that his presence was taking away from his son's im-
mediate source of entertainment, but when he showed
him the shivering finch in his hands, his son dropped
the game controls and moved around the couch to get
a closer look.

"Where did you *find* him?"

"Outside," said Jeremiah. "Come on, let's go out
back. We're gonna set him free."

"You're always catching them."

Jeremiah and his son stood together in the center
of their green lawn, and Jeremiah let him pet the tiny
finch in his hand. Then his son took hold of it.

"Now, before you let it go, say these words with me,
okay?"

"Okay."

"This is a demonstration that we are good, and that
our goodness always trickles down. Are you ready?"

"Yes!"

Together they said the words.

MARIE ANTOINETTE TAKES
AN AFTERNOON AT A WINDOW

Sara grabbed her handbag and started for the door when her husband, Charles, threw his glass of Scotch at the wall near her son's head. It burst like a handful of light bulbs, spraying glass across her boy's face. He squinted, hands up to guard his eyes, and called out, *Mother!* She kept walking, feet moving hard across the brick floor. *You can come if you want,* she said, *or you can stay, but I'm leaving.* The boy looked to both of them, his father kicking wet shards across the floor. He had been given a choice, forced between the two of them. He saw the back of his mother going out of the front door, and he ran after her.

•

Maybe I was too quick. Maybe I could have stayed, could have listened, could have stopped, could have helped pick up, could have listened again, could have gone slower, could have listened some more, could have pulled things farther down, farther, closer to the earth, closer to where we are, closer with no disparity. Have I gone too fast? Should I have taken you with me? You're here and you're helping me, and what can I do about it, now? What can I do about any of it? He threw the glass, threw it right next to your head, and the shards cut you, cut right into you, cut a face he kissed many times, kissed holding you in his arms, in the hospital, in the bedroom, in the bathtub, in the chair, over the crib, for the pictures, and now your face, it's cut-up by the same person, the same man, the one who held us, and we're looking, now we're looking, driving faster than I should, really, like the glass as it flew through the air. Wet night streets, and lamps reflecting back at us with disapproval in their bent shape, disapproval in every-thing, every shape hurtling past our car.

What about that one, Momma? What about those?

No, honey, they look too much like the Psycho motel.

Where are we gonna go, then?

We'll find a place. Sit back, you're too close to the wind-shield.

We stop at Riste's, my friend, my good friend from school, and I tell him everything. He makes a place for us to sleep on a fold out bed. In the middle of the night, with my arm around my son—his eight-year-old face as placid as if he were in his own bed—I struggle on the surface, and squeeze my eyes closed, hoping for rest, and when the sun starts to burst through the windows and shower the room, Riste is on the ground by the pullout bed, his hand inching up my leg, finding me, and I grab his hand, locate the finger and almost break it off, standing up, staring at him. I wake up my son and we're back in the car, leaving Riste's, saying nothing, and my boy is wiping his face, wiping the sleep from his eyes, and we're driving, a return down the streets from last night, and at the end of one of them we pull into a blue motel.

I thought we weren't staying at the Psycho motel?

We are now. Get your things.

•

Sara went back to the house in the evening to pack a bag for herself, and for her son. She named him Justin, but she and Charles took turns renaming him as he got older. Different nicknames stuck: Hoss, Captain, Old Man. Right now, he was only Justin. The situation seemed to demand the severity of actual names. He needed clothes, his toothbrush and other bathroom items, and she needed her own. She cruised down their street like a private detective planning a stakeout, and waited at the curb, checking to make sure Charles hadn't parked in the garage. She didn't see his car in the driveway. The hose in the front yard ran over the roots of the tree closest to the back bedroom. She felt a shattering in her chest looking at it because she knew it wasn't going to be something they shared any longer, a petty thing.

The house seemed empty, so she parked in the driveway and walked across the lawn to turn off the hose before entering. In the foyer there was a stench of something burned, like hair and skin. The air held an electrical quality, a crackle of energy that couldn't escape and hovered just above her as she moved into the living room. On the floor near the windows lay Charles with his shotgun at an angle from his shoulder. His head held the shape of a crescent moon with a jagged red rim. Everything inside his head covered the wall and formed a black pool around him. Sara was immediately reminded of a cherry pie her sisters and her used to eat together as children, how they would split them, breaking them in half, careful not to let the cherries and the syrup get on anything. Nothing of Charles was recognizable, now. Even his body looked withered. It was his clothes and the watch on his wrist, and his hands that gave it away; they made him familiar to her while she stood there looking at him. Hands she had held, and that had held her, that gave so much to both of them.

Her crying was a source of pain itself, barely relieving her of anything. She was momentarily thankful she had left Justin at the hotel room, thinking it would simply be a quick trip, but now it would be much longer. She had no one to call to help her and Riste was out of the question. Her sisters no longer spoke to her, and her parents had passed. If, at any other time, she wished reconciliation were a viable option, it would be now; that she could just call up Julie and Sarah and tell them that their impasse was ridiculous, that they should speak, that her husband was dead, and that he killed himself and she was alone; but none of this would happen. She had betrayed one sister badly enough, sleeping with her husband while visiting. And they all took the side of the betrayed, naturally.

She wasn't sure if it was the helplessness that caused her to start screaming—the sense of cold despair chewing her apart, terror like something crawling around inside her bones—but she howled and howled, one long guttural roar next to the splattered mess that—just hours ago—had been a man she could have helped.

•

Marie Antoinette got bored often. But no one really knew this about her. Very few people (and she was surrounded by many), saw past the well-sculpted mask she presented; that she had to present. She was a person of duties, no matter how much irresponsibility got her wet. But she was bored. And here is a moment of unseen boredom. Of Marie sitting, slightly slumped, at the window of one of her parlors, staring out of the glass at the gardens below.

She held her head up by her right hand, her legs crossed under the many folds of her dress, one of her favorite dresses; and she sat, with no one around, not one person to see her like this, to watch her stare down at her garden, wrapped in the strangely assertive silence of the halls around her. There was a wind that pushed against the glass, but that was the only sound. The rest was only her breathing, the sound of her chest rising and falling, her nostrils taking in the smell of dirt and wood, and the items on her that already included a scent; she perfumed the things that emitted nothing. No one would smell these scents, however, and no one would come upon her this day, catching her while she looked out at the various paths leading away from the fountains. Here, in this space, Marie Antoinette was no one. She was not hated or loved or irresponsible; she did not give parties or hold meetings, or discuss budgets and politics, or budgets and familial bullshit, she was simply a body, an organism that ate, farted, shit, and reeked; a body with orifices that spilled, that hungered, that whined and cried, but could also be silent, very silent; she was made of matter that will rot, does rot, was rotting. None of this is visible, of course; she didn't sit at the window anticipating the guillotine, the dispatching of her head from her gallant, bored shoulders. She had no thought of death in this moment of total ennui, for that's what this was. This time and place with Mme. Antoinette was something no one was privy to; no historian, no dilettante, no fans or sycophants (she knew long before she would be marching up to the giant, slanted blade that historians would want her, all of them; it was inevitable, for she was who she was); but here we're being thoroughly invasive watching her watch this garden, seeing Marie Antoinette luxuriate in her ennui, this cold, stony moment in the padded, round chair by the window.

Her breaths are unobserved by the staff, by her friends (*and what the fuck are those*, she thought). Instead, all of this could be said to be an attempt at altruism; that the only way she could achieve it was to sit here, and watch the sun lower, which it did, and the garden took on purples and blues unobserved by anyone but her. Some orange poured across the horizon, the fields, the poplar trees that stood like good soldiers, militant in their forms. The fountains spouted water silently, changing colors in the light, gaining sharpness as it trickled from the mouths of fish and horns-of-plenty, flowers drooping in perfect, cemented timelessness. A few birds landed on the rim near the water and pecked tentatively near their feet; some jumped in the water, bathing themselves, splashing and then flying off to the trees on the left of the garden and its gray walkways. Marie thought she could see clouds forming over them; a storm was coming, and this created a nostalgic burst of excitement in her, bringing back feelings of girlhood and the storms she pretended scared her, but that she actually enjoyed, wishing privately that the thunder would be hard and heavy enough to rip the whole world apart. She scratched at her head, at the wig pulled tight around it, its weight something she never really got used to despite her years of wearing one. *Fuck this shit,* she thought, wishing to tear it off, because for whose benefit was it, this wig? *Fucking piece of shit. Fuck.*

The birds had gone, and Marie sat in her seat, this tiny, mostly unnoticed chair, staring out of her parlor window until the sun went away, and she was alone in the dark with no one and nothing around her.

•

Sara 's frenetic energy died down after the first three weeks at the hotel. There were a few moments of tears where Justin wanted to return home, but she was amazed at how quickly he adapted to their tiny room and two beds, the plastic cups wrapped in thin, crinkly plastic, the ice bowl and fast food, snack machines, the take-out. People came and went from the hotel, and for the last week it appeared deserted as if they were the only residents to have visited. The woman who ran the front desk smelled of milk and gave off heat the way a drier gives off subtle warmth. Dressed in a gossamer muu-muu, she always conveyed a phoned-in sympathy for Sara and Justin, offering to watch him while she went to take care of some errands, and asking her what she would do until the child returned to school at the end of the summer. Sara accepted one of these offers when she had to deal with the police, make funeral arrangements, and handle the bank regarding the mortgage and the house. She paid to have the carpet professionally cleaned, the rest of the house she cleaned herself, frantically, almost. One day a neighbor came by and left her a plate of cookies and some sandwiches, and offered to help her, for which she was grateful.

Sara consulted realtors and bankers simultaneously. Charles had lost his job and they were behind on the payments, and when she explained this to the bankers, detailing the suicide to emphasize just how badly she needed more time, they did not flinch, they did not squeeze out a tear for her; they gave her dates and amounts. The realtors told her there simply wasn't enough time, and in a fever of delirium, of paranoia, she began to suspect that the realtors and the bank were working together, both giving each other kickbacks off of her loss. One realtor showed some interest, and when Sara took her on a tour of the house, she showed her where they had added equity in the hopes that it would help.

See, this is where Charles built another door to the room in case Justin needed us in the night; he could just access the hallway here instead of going all the way through the living room.

Uh-huh. What a neat addition. Thoughtful.

The trellis in the backyard is where we got married. We built it together, and it has all original woodwork by my husband. You can sand down the notches on the posts if you want, or I can. We each made one to signify the moment. I already painted over the pencil marks in the hallway where we were measuring Justin's growth.

Very good. That's great.

We expanded the living room and the back bedroom, and the ceilings are higher.

Excellent.

The realtor never called Sara back and the house went into foreclosure. The man who processed this called her one afternoon at the hotel to tell her she had twenty-four hours to get every last item that was hers from the property before they prepared it for the next family.

The next family? You already sold it?

The house has been sold, Ma'am.

Our house, it's gone?

It's not your house, and it's not gone. You have twenty-four hours. Do you understand? Workmen will dispose of anything left, permanently.

I can't believe this is happening.

You've had plenty of time, Ma'am.

What does that mean?

Should've paid your mortgage.

Wait a minute…

The man hung up on her. She sat there thinking he had already moved on to another home, another family. The hotel room was quiet. Justin played with some friends he'd made next door. Sara listened to him through the wall.

●

The only people that came to the funeral were friends and family of Charles. They acknowledged Sara briefly, and not too kindly, as they also blamed her for her transgression many years ago. Some, she knew, probably blamed her for his death, for this event, for dragging them out of their homes on a Saturday. She sat alone with Justin in the pew at the front of the church staring at the Urn containing her husband's cremated body. All of him, she thought, shoved into a tiny urn, a whole person compacted, reduced to this. Did he think it would go this way? She wondered. Did he think this is how things would happen?

•

Sara struggled to find work that would take her when her address was a hotel. She also didn't look good. Her physical appearance became wasted, and her hair thinned. Justin had grown despondent and rarely reacted when she tried to do something cheerful for the both of them. She had some money remaining from the insurance policy, but most of it went to paying off lawyers and funeral costs. Very little was left and soon she would have to do something. Justin was about to start school, and he needed things.

A week later a bar within walking distance took her on a temporary basis waiting tables. She got two dollars an hour, and there was tip-share. Some of the waitresses had been there a few years and were not kind to her, but they didn't try to sabotage her, either. A few weeks into the job and she was a little better than some of the others, making enough money to buy her son's supplies, and maybe something he really wanted, like a toy, something. The routine of the job numbed her, and one night an older patron gave her a ten-dollar tip. He smiled at her like a preacher.

On the receipt, he wrote her a note. It said: *This is to show you that people are mostly good. And, in a forgiving world, God exits. And it surely is a forgiving world.*

Sara took the tip but didn't say anything.

•

Sara returned home from work one night around 2:00 AM. The hotel room was empty. She went to the front desk, and the woman in her muu-muu said she hadn't seen Justin, nor had she heard anything. Sara went down the row of doors, knocking on each one, and the ones that opened, sleepy-eyed and frightened, said they hadn't seen or heard anything, either. She peered into these other rooms, looking for him, and they became impatient with her. She called the police, begging them for help, ashamed at her shaking voice, and holding onto the edge of her bed while the officer took down notes. She gave them a picture of Justin, and something in the act caused her a ripple of pain that underscored the present moment.

We'll look for him, Ma'am. Try to take it easy.

Okay, okay.

Sara did not sleep. She stared out of the window. She stared for a long time and wanted to know who was looking back at her because she felt that someone was. Even if no one was there, someone was there. That's how she saw it.

Who sees me? She asked. *Who sees me from another place? Who's watching me?*

She got a call from her boss at 6:00 AM. One of the girls had quit, could she come in to cover her? Sara said Justin was missing, that she shouldn't leave in case he came back.

I'm real sorry to hear that, said her boss. *Do ya like your job?*

I'm a mother first, she thought.

Is that a yes or a no?

Sara got dressed, taking her time. The sun came over the trees and turned the sky pale, then she walked to work.

●

Today, Mme. Antoinette chose the same window, but a different chair. This chair was made of a deep burgundy silk. The bloody color of it felt warm to Marie. She took her original position near the sill, staring out at the same garden. The light was filtered through an overcast sky, clouds breaking only momentarily to show her the unfettered blue underneath. She wasn't sure if she wanted the clouds to remain, or to break away entirely to reveal something. She felt their presence was important somehow.

The salon was empty again, as were the rest of that wing, and that hall. The garden was the same as it had been the previous day when she sat in her boredom, watching the light play over the walkways, the various paths among hedges and, of course, the fountain with its birds. She noticed that there were fewer birds today. The fountain appeared abandoned as if the birds had found another place to wash and splash. Perhaps there weren't enough insects for them to gobble, thought Marie, who leaned closer to the windowpane, legs crossed under her dark-blue dress. She reached forward with her hand and touched the glass of the window. In doing this, the space became solid. Before touching the window, the absolute vacuum of sound had dissolved her sense of self save for the wind pushing against the building and the other windows. The room was stripped of definition. She enjoyed that it could be any room, not just this one in this wing. By touching the cool glass, the room fell under her control; it was entirely hers, as was the silence it offered, and its emptiness.

Less bored today, Marie really observed the garden this time, rather than passively glaring at it. She saw it as a miniature theater presenting to her a packaged unpredictability; something might happen, or something might not, and the garden would stay the same. She waited for it to reveal something to her, something unpredictable, and for a while there was nothing. *Things can happen simultaneously*, she thought. *Time isn't what we think it is.*

Eventually one of her groundskeepers could be seen in the distance moving about the poplars and the hedges, completely unaware of Marie watching him. She wondered if his unawareness of her at the window made him more entertaining. *I could masturbate*, she thought. *I could press myself to this window, pulling on myself, smashing my white breasts against the glass, bringing myself off. No one would know. Who would see?* For a minute she thought of doing this; that it was somehow necessary when a flicker of movement caught her eye at the lower edge of the window.

Between the tallest hedges stared the red face of a fox, its determined eyes directed somewhere across the courtyard. It felt safe where it was hidden in the shadows under the hedgerows, stealthy in its approach. It stepped forward a little bit more, and its golden eyes caught some of the light. Marie steadied herself on the edge of the chair, hands at her throat, waiting. The groundskeeper was gone and the courtyard was empty. The sun lowered and the fox became a shadow. She couldn't spot him anymore, but she felt him there, both looking at each other through the glass.

ACKNOWLEDGMENTS

I want to thank the incredible team at Spuyten Duyvil Press, who opened their doors to me by publishing my first novel with such kindness and receptivity to the process and by showing me that a home for my work was possible. I am also very grateful to Dr. Sara Veglahn who understood what I was trying to accomplish with much of the writing in these stories. Both Dr. Veglahn's guidance and the strong insights of Lewis Warsh helped me find the right notes and to unveil the natural direction for the title story, "Consummation." I am also thankful to Anne Waldman and Riki Ducornet for their input and discussions, especially when it comes to following paths that veer. Many friends over the years have taken the time to give me their viewpoints on my writing, and my gratitude is infinite. I am thankful for any friends or family who took a moment out of their lives to indulge me when I wanted to test an idea. My immeasurable gratitude also goes to one of my writing heroes, Michael Cunningham, and The Iowa Writers' Workshop for publishing *The Exchange* on NPR, an amazing moment in my life, many moons ago.

Blake Edward Hamilton holds an MFA in Creative Writing from Naropa University. His work has appeared in World Literature Today Magazine: Windmill, NPR, Bombay Gin Literary Journal, The Guerrilla Lit Mag., and South Broadway Press, among others. He is the author of the novel, *Hiraeth*, and the collections of poetry *All Through Your Multiple Selves* and *Move In Silence*.